messages in a small town

Nancy Davies

Published by Nouveau Proletariat Press
nouveauproletariat.com

ISBN-13: 978-0692537527

contents

Stories

the journey

One would not think of Mexico as an ideal place to die, despite the lure of its endless high mountains. Certainly Jim had not come here seeking death, not his own nor Todd's. And yet the landscape offered space for death, as it offered space for life.

Braced elbows on knees on the carved wood chair, he gazed at the form beneath a thin blanket. The climate, burning by day, cooled at night. It was now 1:00 A.M., air lurked at the window, waiting to wash the room. Todd, wrapped in the woven striped cotton, stirred. Jim would not open the windows. Todd's morphine coma did not forget a scratching and digging at his skin, as if the senseless fingers went on about their daily tasks without Todd's input. Todd moved an arm, and slept.

Jim on his chair by the closed window yearned for the breeze held out by the glass. So many things held at bay by a transparent thin sheet of glass. As if life, passing by a window, could be observed forever at a distance.

But somehow had gotten in. Entered into the space vacated by Todd's leaving home. The boy's leaving had opened a wall, not just a window. Forever open, as Jim glared and denied clichés of waiting, a candle in the window, an empty mailbox, virgin snow, while his boy strode through the world without a backward glance.

And then came back. And was ill.

Jim denied. The death of his wife Gladys, so many months of pain and waiting before her release. Wrapped in a hospital sheet, on a hospital bed placed in the living room on top of the spruce green carpet she purchased when Todd was born, because she feared the boy might crack his head on the hard linoleum covering a cement base. The house was Levittown, prefab, precision-cut in the factory. Men came and seized numbered boxes. Their home wasn't built, it was assembled. Panels representing walls were carried from the truck to a concrete base poured the previous week to accept their living room, their PVC pipes for plumbing, their wires for electricity. What they could afford, and hadn't they thrilled to own a house, and bring their baby home to it from the hospital. And before Todd could master his bowed legs, she bought the carpet on monthly payments, to protect him. Gladys used mother's instincts right from the get-go. She hated to die. She judged herself as abandoning her two men, although Todd was long gone. With no way to lure him. She fretted. He'll be back you'll see and then what? she demanded. He'll want to see me and I won't be here! For a long while she determined to stay, to be right available when he returned, but he didn't come in time; the cancer took her. And now Todd.

Todd returned home after his own cancer was well along. He greeted his father and almost immediately suffered a seizure and thudded onto the green carpet bought to protect him thirty-five years before. Jim held his son and wondered briefly how he could go through it again. He had help to care for Gladys because she wanted to die at home. But it took so long, and after the day nurse welcomed him home from the office and left, Jim pretty much lived through motions not his own. Finally the hospice service insisted he accept a second shift to watch over her while Jim slept. So obediently Jim slept. But he didn't sleep well, he slept listening for the sound that would indicate his wife was dead.

What sound would that be? The nurse dialing the hospice doctor who would come to confirm? Or the sound of the nurse's gasp, when she realized she had dozed and her patient had died. Or the sound of Gladys calling, calling out her last words, as if they could have been more than whisper, a whispered demand that Jim be there at her side when she crossed over.

Could he endure that again? The silence and waiting, the last bite of food gotten down, the last tube dripping fluids, the last bedpan removed, the sheet changed, the patient's back washed and rubbed. The dead flesh.

Todd wanted to live, just as his mother had wanted to. When he could sit and speak Todd told his father people spoke of a treatment in Mexico. In a place named Tepetzcoco, a remote mountain town where a curandero did wonders with herbs only the indigenous ancients knew. He wanted to go. The doctors in California had given up. Yes he'd been in California. Jim didn't ask why Todd went there, or what he'd been doing for the past fifteen years. Apparently he wasn't married. Apparently he wasn't in prison or bad trouble. In Jim's mind traveling as far as California was a mythic event, like riding out on quest. A young man by predestination went to California; California called like God calling him to serve, that his children abandon dreary winters in Ohio and dreary parents in their pre-fab house. Of course. They heard the summons and complied, through the gaping wall cut in the pre-fab house, with no more gear than backpack and a handshake. Todd informed his parents: he wanted to go. He had to go. He took his Giants baseball cap. That hat and that backpack were of Jim's giving. His other possessions Todd left behind, the Beatles albums and the dozen issues of Hot Rod magazine.

Did they all come home to die? Did they need to die with mom and dad close by, in the other reality of life, the unsummoned; the patient endurance of life measured by seasons, first there's spring, and then summer; leaves fall and then comes snow, and then spring emerges, followed by summer. So lived the ones who never leave. Todd had been the voyager, the one so different from them they knew no measure for his energy or search. Only when he was very small and climbed out of his cot and found their bed. Beneath the quilt Jim felt the hot small body of his son, and sang out to him Here's my hot Toddy! The small Todd would vanish beneath the cover and emerge at the foot of the bed, exposing Jim's awkward feet to the air. Until finally Gladys would swing out her side of the bed and heft the child under her arm. Off to change his wet diaper, eat breakfast, flop in front of the cartoon TV and drum his small hot feet on the carpet bought for his safety.

Todd had some money, saved from his work in California. His health insurance had carried him through months of radiation and chemo. Now he wanted to take his remaining cash and go to Mexico. For a cure. He was certain it would work. Only he suffered seizures now, and needed some assistance. Where was his mother? But she was dead. Jim flung into the mailbox Christmas cards that Todd hardly ever acknowledged. Gladys sent him birthday cards, but last year no cards sought his latest address, not from Gladys and not from Jim. Todd never emerged from his California dream long enough to worry about his parents during those fifteen years, if indeed he received their reminders. What was Jim to say? How could he explain that the life Todd fled also was real, and passed through time as relentlessly as the quest-life of California. In California time only seemed to remain stationary, but then one day a person could wake up with a brain tumor and seizures, or worse yet, with a dull job and dingy apartment too far from the beach. Jim waited for Todd to say he grasped this truth, but Todd said almost nothing. Only that he wanted to go. To go again. This time to Mexico. This time with his father to help him. Todd left his backpack and Giants baseball cap on the floor in the living room and groped his way along the wall into the room that had been his bedroom. He slept a lot these days.

The next morning Jim retired from his job. He could do that, an early retirement. He cashed out, that was what they called it. He took his pension and arranged the automatic deposits with his bank. He obtained a passport. Todd already carried one. It was part of California, Jim knew without asking. Naturally Todd had a passport, although his father age sixty-three had not left the country since military service forty years ago. Didn't want to. Wanted only to be in his neat house with his wife and watch his son grow. His hot Toddy. His green carpet baby.

Todd roused himself to purchase airline tickets. Jim watched as Todd sat across from him at the Formica table to eat, and often did. Jim watched Todd drink his milk as carefully as he did when Gladys said Be careful now don't spill use two hands. Todd used two hands. The flight would take them to Mexico City. From there they would ride buses. Jim counted his cash reserves. Hotel rooms, fares and food were cheap in Mexico.

The trip from the vast city to southern countryside unrolled as the bus rolled, while scenery moved backward past the window. The buses seemed to be part of a dream in which one travels in silver and blue seats forever, over endless roads abutting looming mountains. They slept and woke. One night Todd suffered another seizure and for many of the hours on the bus he dozed. Jim hoped with no hope. He didn't hope that Todd would survive. He hoped Todd would speak to him about what it meant to be a quest person, to leave home and never look back. Rarely respond to greeting cards. Always signed "with love" but never a visit. Step out into another world like that. Jim wasn't hurt or angry. He wanted only to understand what it was, that urgent need pushing his migratory son onward, with no time to look back.

Finally they arrived. They took two rooms in the small hotel although Jim wanted to sleep in the same room. But two rooms gave them each a respite. Jim hoped he would hear if Todd fell onto the bare tile floor. The walls were thick, old style adobe. Probably he would be as far from Todd as if Todd were in California. No communication. But he agreed. Todd, reed-thin and wobbling, owned the quest. Todd inquired of the local people. Todd followed their instructions to find the house of the curandero along a cactus-fenced road of the village. Beside towering pipe organ plants Todd paid the taxi and requested a return pickup.

The curandero of Tepetzcoco took Todd between his brown knobby hands. He massaged Todd's head and gave him a scalding green broth to drink and then a chilled red liquid. He blew smoke at him and waved it away with branches of sage. Jim watched. Todd nodded as he surrendered to the process. He floated in a reality different from the reality Jim, watching his son, knew. The reality Jim knew was that doctors cut off or cut out everything they could and then recommended hospice care. The reality Jim knew was the sickening radiation and chemotherapy Todd had followed as carefully as Gladys did before him. Gladys's hair grew back and Todd's hair grew back.

Jim knew that reality. He knew it in his speechless bones, the weight and consistency of that reality. Now Todd's reality tried to fill this room. The quest for a cure, the journey to faraway corners where the air suffocated them hot and dry until the first hours of morning. Todd's reality struggled to find a footing, a place to heal, to live.

Jim wondered if he should be grateful that Todd came home to seek his assistance. Jim wondered if he should be grateful for the opportunity to partner a quester, or if he should be grateful to sit with his son while his son died, as he had been with his wife. In point of fact Gladys had died mid-morning while Jim worked at the office.

The nurse telephoned and he drove home promptly. Gladys lay on her back with her grey hair neatly combed. Her nightgown was fresh and still showed creases from the laundry. Jim had not been present. But he felt as if he had been. It was more of the same, her death, more of their reality. The doctor came and signed papers. The body was driven to a crematorium. The ashes were delivered into Jim's hands, in a small cedar box. Jim didn't know what to do with the box. He still hadn't decided when Todd arrived. He didn't tell Todd the box of his mother's ashes rested on the shelf of the hall closet.

Jim wondered what he would do with Todd's body. Seated in the hotel room as Todd slept under the morphine provided by the town's doctor he realized that he spoke no Spanish. The doctor had been summoned by a net flung into the air, by the curandero Jim supposed, who knew that death was certain and that an official doctor would be necessary. The doctor knocked on the door of the hotel room in which Jim usually slept when he was not sitting near his son. Jim understood the doctor's small black bag. He ushered the doctor to the adjacent room.

The doctor looked at Todd and raised Todd's eyelid. He said something in Spanish to Jim, and Jim nodded. He didn't know what the doctor said but clearly it didn't matter. Neither Jim nor the doctor were in California. The doctor injected Todd with some liquid in a syringe. The curandero came later and burned sage and waved away the smoke. The room filled with a scent like California under the hot sun in the desert. Jim had never been there, but he imagined. Despite his life of reality he was not lacking imagination. So he wondered what he would do when Todd was dead.

At the event he went down to the hotel desk. They were waiting. The doctor was summoned and signed some papers. The curandero took charge of the body, washing Todd and wrapping him in a fresh, clean mantle of cream-colored cotton, heavy and perfect like a bride's dress. Jim waited in the other room, his room. From no direction a coffin arrived and Todd was lifted into it. Jim stayed in his room, resting on the covered mattress. The bed consisted of a rough wood frame, a mattress lying on its wood platform offered a surprisingly comfortable rest. Jim was tired, so he rested.

When he finally got up and went down to the lobby the coffin was being led away by the curandero and a group of musicians. The musicians dressed alike in green shirts and black trousers, and this must be their work. Most men had left the town, maybe hundreds, seeking a place in California where God lived. With their brass instruments the musicians repeated a stubborn view. Jim understood the declaratory music, Here we stay, and walked behind the coffin of his son carried by four men. They moved slowly. The cemetery occupied the end of the town's one paved street, four rows of crosses and headstones, photos, wilted flowers or bleached plastic, all displayed in clay urns. Jim watched the men lower the coffin from their shoulders into the earth already dug and waiting. The musicians repeated their tune, something with a drum and two horns, unchanging in its rhythm, rooted, obdurate.

When the burial was complete Jim paid the musicians. He paid the doctor, the priest and the men who carried his son's coffin. He paid the curandero, for what service he didn't know, but perhaps some participation with Todd. He paid the waiting carpenter for the rude coffin, now out of sight with Todd beneath the dust-colored earth.

Finally he returned to their rooms and made ready to leave. He put Todd's Giants cap into Todd's backpack and left the rest of Todd's clothing in the wardrobe. He took his own duffel bag and added to his clothes the backpack with the baseball cap inside. On second thought he opened the backpack and withdrew the cap and placed it on his own head.

He descended the stairs to the hotel desk and counted out pesos for the waiting bill. He walked to the bus stop and waited outside in the heavy sun for a bus to Mexico City. A long ride lay ahead and he hoped he would sleep as he made his way back north.

teaching hortencia

I stopped in at the American library, and while I waited in front of the checkout desk I ran into Pat, who's been running the place since the board made Ruth retire on her fiftieth anniversary. I like Pat, she carries a lot of defiant hair spread around her head and shoulders. I told her, "Lately I'm accepting free any student who really needs English," and she said, Great.

While this conversation was concluding, Junie Alice approached us. Her Mexican ribbon-striped Mixteca dress and her short dyed-black hair give me a pain, I better admit that right up front. Before I cast any aspersions on Junie Alice you'll know I didn't like her in the first place. Nor her husband, I might add. They're retired Liberals and retired Liberals give me a pain.

Like Junie Alice told me, they don't read the news any more. I guess they found out bad things happen from the USA, despite their many years dedicated to liberal politics. Getting out the vote, so much effort, all for this. So they quit and came to Mexico for the winter, nothing gets done in the summer anyway. Here they're still liberals; excuse me, I don't mean they've turned fascist, even though she gives me a pain.

Junie Alice hired a Mexican maid to clean and do laundry. The woman's name is Hortencia, and she's maybe forty years old, and Junie Alice thinks her husband drinks and knocks her around. Instant sympathy. Righteous indignation. All that.

So Junie Alice intruded on my conversation in front of the checkout desk with Pat, and asked me Could I teach her maid Hortencia to read and write? Like a fool, right off I said Sure, and Junie Alice told me to come around to her place in the late afternoon when Hortencia would be finished defrosting the refrigerator, and we could get acquainted. My brain was almost in gear, so I asked Junie Alice to check around the library for anything in Spanish that would be okay, because for sure I wasn't going to teach Hortencia to read English.

My brain was really in gear by the time I arrived back at our apartment. For instance, I asked Bert—although just rhetorically— can Hortencia see, or does she have middle-aged vision, because nobody's going to buy her reading glasses? Has she ever been tested for dyslexia, or something like that? Junie Alice told me Hortencia never went to school, like many poor people hereabouts; she didn't tell me if Hortencia had other problems; I mean other than having two teenage kids and a husband who knocks her around. Finally I decided I would try not to be too embarrassed, and just wing it.

Thursday is Hortencia's regular day to clean Junie Alice's apartment. I knocked around 3:30.

Hortencia was wearing a homemade turquoise sheath dress and plastic shoes. Her black hair was tied back in a pony tail. Junie Alice was wearing a gaily-colored Zapoteca blouse over her slacks. I was wearing – well, of course you don't care what I was wearing! This is absurd. Anyway, I was wearing jeans.

Junie Alice called Hortencia from her work, and left the two of us alone together sitting on the balcony. Junie Alice decorated the balcony with lots of potted palms and cactuses and bougainvillea, but it's still a balcony overlooking a parking lot. It was quiet below, no cars moving. I could focus on Hortencia. Junie Alice brought several books in Spanish from the library, like Goldipelo y Los Tres Osos. And a counting book for numbers, in English, but Junie Alice quickly pointed out that Arabic numerals are the same in both languages.

I smiled at Hortencia who gave a nice smile right back, and first off I wanted to know if her vision was okay; I asked her if she could see the letters on the cover of a paperback Mario Puzo that John was reading and she said she could. She lost his place but I figured that wasn't my problem.

Then I took out my little notebook and drew some sticks and circles, to see if she was dyslexic. I made a vertical stick with a circle attached on its left side, and a vertical stick with a circle attached on its right side. I asked Hortencia if she could see which side the circle was on, and she replied without shutting down her sweet smile, Si, es letra d, y la otra es letra b.

To make a long humiliating story short, it turns out that Hortencia knows the alphabet, and can read. She reads the Bible every day on the bus to her cleaning jobs because she's Evangelical. She knows the numbers too, because she refers to chapter and verse.

At this point I flat asked her how come Junie Alice believed that Hortencia can't read, and it seems Hortencia told Junie Alice that Hortencia had gone to school only two years, and from that came Junie Alice's false conclusion.

We chatted awhile, and Hortencia told me her teenagers are in Secondario and doing fine. She has two Evangelical women friends who might like to come to read the Bible with me and her. They hardly went to school either.

Hortencia went back into the apartment to finish up. Junie Alice emerged onto the balcony. She asked me how it went, because she heard us laughing and supposed we got on well? Yes, really well, I said, and by the way, Hortencia can read and write. That's amazing, Junie Alice said, you must be a miracle worker.

Well, Junie Alice, I admitted, she could actually read and write all along. Junie Alice was surprised as all getout, and told me Hortencia's husband really kicked her around when he was drunk. Junie Alice said she put a bruise on her own thigh from walking into a coffee table, and when she showed it to Hortencia, Hortencia hitched up her dress and showed Junie Alice a bruise THIS LONG. So that's how Junie Alice knows her husband is a drunkard.

Anyway, I said, getting ready to leave, if Hortencia wants to walk with me I'll show her where I live. She can stop by after work some day to read the Bible with me. I didn't see any point in making Junie Alice feel bad, despite my not liking her. Junie Alice said That would be fine, and from now on she was going to leave lists of tasks for Hortencia, well, today she already defrosted the refrigerator, but maybe next week like "wash the floor". I agreed Junie Alice could do that; because practicing writing in Spanish would do her good. Junie Alice's accent is horrible but lots of people write and read a foreign language better than they speak it.

Hortencia changed from her plastic shoes into her leather ones, and after carefully folding Junie Alice's laundry, led the way down the steps through the parking lot to the street. We headed north, and Hortencia told me she comes this way all the time, because she shops at the market up here before catching the bus home. When we arrived at my street corner I pointed, You'll know this is my street because, look across, there's a sign on that building.

Oh, sure, says Hortencia, Registro Civil.

We turned left. At my door I told Hortencia she was welcome to come by any time. She nodded and smiled. She passes my front door frequently on her way to buy vegetables. And she'll bring her Bible.

I unlocked my door and went in. Bert was home, so I told him what happened. He just laughed at how mad I was and suggested maybe I could help out the women by reading alternatively a chapter of Bible and a paragraph of Flores Magón, who is Bert's favorite Mexican anarchist.

Maybe. Hortencia's pretty nice, so probably she won't ever show up. She'll take the six dollars a day Junie Alice pays her and share it with the drunkard husband. She's nice because of religion.

The next night I got an e-mail from Pat, who asked me if I would accept a student who really does need English. She wrote I could come by the library to meet the young woman, who's there pretty early Mondays and Wednesdays because she's also the library's cleaning lady. But if I wanted a direct introduction, I should come this week, because Pat handed in her resignation at the library. Ruth is still on tap.

So I e-mailed back and told her, give the girl my name and address. I can manage the rest.

the dogs were barking

The dogs were barking again. They looked downward through the darkness to the street below and barked crazily, running back and forth along the parapet, unable to do more than bark. Who was walking by? Guendolín supposed it was as always, a passerby on the way to the bus stop.

Every night these accursed dogs barked. At two A.M. Guendolín came awake to listen and mutter imprecations. One dog yapped in a high voice, two others were bass. She wondered if on the street anybody else woke when these dogs barked. And if not, what good were they? Nobody would respond if a thief entered a house. And the owners, did they waken? And so what if their dogs barked? Did they leap from their beds to see who was stealing the fence?

Guendolín lay alone on her side of the bed and muttered dark words to the dark night. Outside her window stars lurked, but she kept them hidden by curtains. Fresh air swirled below the moon, but she shut it out with the window. There were forgotten songs and suitors, but these were not near enough even to make dogs bark. Accursed dogs.

Guendolín pulled the blanket higher around her chin.

In the daylight the dogs barked even more frequently, because now many people climbed the street to the bus stop, or left the bus to descend to the market below. Her life on the street had changed since the bus began. Women passed with baskets and bags on their heads, students passed carrying their mochillos jammed with heavy books. They laughed and spoke entirely too loudly, oblivious of Guendolín in her patio or the dogs on their roof. The cacophonous street plagued her soul, or her head, or her back.

Guendolín watched the students stride uphill toward their university. This was also new. The students appeared clean and well-fed. Indeed, so did she. Despite her widowhood and meager pension, she washed and ate also. Gracias a Diós. She was healthy also, and had lost only two teeth, both after she had nursed her children. And those ungrateful sons, where were they? In what part of the world? Certainly not here, skipping up the hill toward a university. She turned her mouth in a bitter grimace, and took from a wicker basket the gardening tools she used. She pulled on the yellow leather gloves, and set her hat firmly on her faded hair to keep off the bright sun, although at nine o'clock sunlight barely strolled over the roof. Guendolín was somewhat fair of skin, not a blanca, but in her ancestry more than one such bequeathed her rose-tinged complexion, hair more brown than black, and a strange name. How her husband had admired her skin. In the first year of their marriage he whispered to her, "I am the color of earth, and your blush salutes me like the first light of dawn." An extravagant man. And she was tall, too, strong and healthy with her faint rose cheeks. He wanted her to bring him children. She was a simple woman with faith in the saints and the Virgin. The soil she loved to tend was as brown as her husband. So she agreed. She prayed only briefly, and with each new child she was delighted. But where were those ungrateful children now? In what part of the world? Furthermore, her husband was dead. And in what part of

God's world was he? Not in the blue heaven, she hoped. He cheated on her too many times for salvation! Well, perhaps in the heaven of his ancestors, those ancient people the first on Mexican earth. They knew gods before God arrived, and remained faithful to those gods in some part of their being hidden to Guendolín. For that reason her husband was a good man, he didn't beat her or the children. Simply, he had an extravagant eye. Aye, Diós.

She bent over the garden, loosening the soil around the pretty paragüitas, cursing the weeds like she cursed the dogs, wondering if she could divide the sweet patch of oregano, now twice the size of when she planted it.

"Señora."

Guendolín looked up, and straightened her back carefully. Some days it straightened easily, other days with great difficulty. It was better to use caution. A boy stood at her gate.

"Dígame."

"I can help you in your garden. I can cut the dry branches and pull the weeds." The boy held up pruning shears for her to see. Well, she had pruning shears herself. The dogs continued barking, and she cupped her hand over her ear. "I can't hear you! Those accursed dogs!"

The boy gazed at her quietly. He was wearing a blue jersey torn on one shoulder, loose cotton pants. On his chin a scar. He should be in school at this hour, but clearly was not. Aye, Diós. Perhaps he attended the afternoon session, after morning labor.

Guendolín opened the gate and beckoned. It was necessary to retreat three meters to be able to speak over the barking. "I can help you," the boy repeated. "You can pay me whatever you choose."

The boy looked thin, not so strong. Guendolín didn't need help. But the boy needed help, that was clear. Where in the world now were her own boys?

"What's your name?"

"Cosi."

"And what work does your father do?"

"I'm an orphan," the boy said. "My father died and my mother also."

"Who do you live with?"

"My grandmother."

"And where is that?"

"On Monte Alban."

It was not necessary for Guendolín to think hard to understand the grandmother was poor. The tourists who went to Monte Alban saw only the grand ruins, but in the present day those who resided on the hillside of Monte Alban were poor, many with no cement floors, nor bathrooms or kitchens indoors. It was not necessary to think too hard to know the grandmother sent the boy to work each morning because school cost money for enrollment and a uniform. Perhaps they even needed the money he earned in order to eat. Perhaps the grandmother kept a garden for food?

Yes, Cosi helped his grandmother in the garden, and he liked to garden. He liked the earth. He like the color and he liked to smell it and feel it. Guendolín briefly recalled her husband. As for Cosi, she could see some of his passion beneath his fingernails, a dark rim on each finger.

"And when you are a man, what will you do?"

"I will be a biologist," he responded. "Putting seeds in the soil and bringing plants out of the soil." Guendolín supposed that to be a biologist required long years of education. Although many of these country boys learned plants as they learned to speak, effortlessly. As she herself had learned from her parents and then from her husband. However, science was something different! The boy appeared to have about ten years, but hardly cast a thin, small shadow.

"I need some sand," Guendolín told him finally. "For the cactus I am planting." On a whim she had bought in the Friday market a tiny cactus in bloom with a bright speck of orange flower which looked plastic but in fact was real, stuck like a button on the rim of a pad of nopal. In what mood had she spent good money on something so small and so pretty! So useless! But now that she owned it, she was obliged to care for it, just like the owners of those fool dogs must feed them.

"I'll bring you sand," the boy said.

About an hour later the boy returned with a plastic bag. It was heavy, sand is not light, and she thought the boy might be uneasy with hunger. But she said only, "How much?" And Cosi repeated, "Whatever you think best."

"Help me then." She handed him the small cactus in its tin container made from half a beer can. "Here's where I want to plant it." She indicated the bright sun that now covered half the garden like a sheet of light.

Cosi carefully took hold of the cactus with an old newspaper. He shook it out of its tin and gently spread its roots.

Guendolín watched his neat hands and fingers as brown as if working with the soil had colored them. Cosi dug an area and filled it with soil and sand, mixed together. He set the cactus into the place and covered the roots snugly like a baby in bed, with soil and sand on top. All this he did flawlessly, with no visible effort, bending his black head and brown face over the tiny plant. Guendolín guessed he knew this from his grandmother, or from living on Monte Alban, a high rolling landscape where cactus and other wild plants jutted from the soil. She liked the idea of a wild garden, that only nature tended. Each year she was more stiff in her bones. Nobody was here to help. God alone knew where in the world her children were these past twenty years, who should be here to assist her. Now there was only this thin ragged boy. She took from her apron pocket a tiny purse and gave the boy ten pesos.

"I'll come tomorrow and help you?" This was a question.

"Let me think, "Guendolín replied. She didn't know if the boy would return or not, nor what she would do if he did.

The next morning at nine o'clock she found him perched like a bird on the wall beside the gate. Between his knees rested another plastic bag which sagged as if it was filled with rocks.

"Good morning, boy. What do you have in that bag?"

"Good morning, Señora. I have some rocks for you." So indeed the child carried rocks. He brought his bag through the gate and carefully reached into it, not turning out the rocks onto the ground by tipping the bag. No, he reached into the bag and took each separately and carefully, as if he were pulling small animals out of a box, or something very precious and expensive. But they were only rocks.

"And what is so special about these rocks?"

"They are rocks of Monte Alban." Guendolín looked at the boy and looked at the rocks. So that was significant? She wondered why, but did not ask. Her right hand twitched as if she would make the sign of the cross, but she did not. Instead she said, "Ah," a comment which always served to disguise confusion.

The boy began to rake the soil of the garden until it was clean and flat. He began to work without asking or speaking, as if already told to prepare this soil. Then he lay down the rocks. There were only four, heavy and blue. They were rough and irregular in shape, not smooth at all, but an unusual shade of blue, like the boy's torn shirt, the same shirt he wore yesterday. Perhaps he had no other.

Cosi placed the rocks in a straight line precisely on the line drawn by the roof separating sun from shade. The stones seemed to divide the sun from shade but that was foolishness because Guendolín had bent here every day since the day of her marriage, and the line dividing shade from sun moved precisely with the seasons, each year always the same. On the adobe and cement houses, on the cobbled street, on the small gardens, on the flat roofs, always the same.

Nevertheless the rocks seemed significant, so neatly half bright and half dull. Therefore Guendolín said, "Ah." She reached into her purse. She gave the boy five pesos only, because after all he did nothing but place stones in a line.

Cosi pocketed the five pesos coin. "Tomorrow I'll bring more."

But why, Guendolín wanted to ask. What were these rocks good for? Were they magic? For a moment she thought perhaps they were, because as if a miracle had taken place the dogs had fallen silent and were visible on the far roof lying down like lambs.

Nevertheless in the night Guendolín woke as usual and cursed the barking dogs. Fortunately they barked only briefly, and after a few moments she returned to sleep, and resumed her dream. In this dream one of her sons was standing in front of their house wearing a blue shirt. She noticed in the dream how straight his shoulders looked, as if placed in a line. That must be the oldest, Pepe, who had gone for the United States when no more than seventeen. Many nights Guendolín dreamed of Pepe because in her heart she feared he was dead, and that only her mother's dream would retain his spirit and hold it like a seed from blowing away to the sky. Why he had gone, there was no good answer. They all went, it was the thing to do, to find adventure and earn big American money. At first the father said, "This is your birthplace, here. You come of the earth and sunrise here." He appeared troubled. But later when the boys, now become men, persisted he said nothing, merely shrugged his acquiescence. Guendolín would have shouted No! but it was not permitted to do so. Instead of shouting she wrung her hands in her apron. Some men who went returned, with or without money, and some never were heard from again. Guendolín rolled onto her side and pulled the cover up around her ear.

In the morning she drank her chocolate and wondered if the boy Cosi would come, and if he came would he like some warm chocolate in a bowl with sweet bread to dip. Most likely this small gift would not be unwelcome, and when the boy arrived Guendolín placed the warm bowl and bread outside on the small patio table. Cosi carried another plastic sack which he set down carefully while he drank and chewed. Guendolín contained her curiosity. The boy wiped his mouth with the back of his hand the way boys will, and smiled.

The sack held twenty little stones, as small as vertebrae. Guendolín saw the rocks were round and pale. Cosi placed them carefully in a straight line perpendicular to the blue rocks. They were in the sun, and if rocks can appear happy these enjoyed the warmth and soaked up life. This time Guendolín gave the boy ten pesos, because after all he had placed more stones.

And so it continued. Each night Guendolín dreamed of one of her missing sons; the four of them had gone and vanished forever but not from her web of dreams. Each day the boy arrived with stones from the ancient hill of Monte Alban. Guendolín dared say nothing as the stone figure appeared in her garden. Yes, she said nothing but yes, clearly it was a figure created from stone. The four blue rocks were the shoulders, the twenty pale stones were the spine. And then the boy brought five brown stones for the right arm with an elbow, and then five brown stones for the left arm with an elbow. The legs appeared, and then feet. By now a month had passed, the rocks were heavy for the boy to carry, and he carried no more than he could carry. Also he must spend time searching, because although Monte Alban was covered with careless stones, they must match and be of the correct color. When finally Cosi placed the head it was clearly the head of her second son Ferd, who had the round tan face of a good rock. When Cosi placed the hands they were clearly the two hands, right and left, of her third son Luis, whose hands were freckled and clumsy as stones. And the fourth boy, her youngest and dearest, ah finally, Cosi brought tiny many-colored pebbles which created his belt. Of all her boys only the youngest wore a beaded belt, which he proudly bought at the market so he could hang his thumbs the way older boys did.

At night when the dogs did not bark Guendolín slept dreaming of one son after the other, all of them vanished, all restored beneath Cosi's labor in her garden. The stone face enjoyed the shade as was appropriate, and the body soaked up the sun. Finally there was nothing more to do. Cosi came with the plastic sack and drank the offered bowl of chocolate. This time the sack contained four rosy pink stones. Cosi knelt carefully and placed them in a cluster beneath the four blue-shirt stone rocks. So there were four hearts in the one body, just as four dreams resided in the one mother.

Then Guendolín wanted to know what she could do with these four-boys-in-one stone sons, or what they could do with her. She gazed at the thick agave and thin dedos de cristo which surrounded them, sprung out of the soil with no help from her hands, as if to welcome the returned boys. The round plants clustered in curious shades of green to view them, snug in their garden like babes in a cradle. The stone four-boys-in-one lay in the garden on the line dividing sun and shade, and faced upward to the sky, smiling at their father. This of course was merely her imagination, because the head was created only by one unwinking round brown stone. But so it seemed.

And what shall I do with this stone four-boys-in-one?" she finally asked the boy Cosi. But he just shook his dark head. He accepted his final payment which was four pesos, since he brought only four pink stones. "Goodbye, Señora. I have finished with this garden. May all go well with you."

In her kitchen Guendolín shed a few tears after Cosi walked back up the hill toward the bus stop. She had become fond of his company each morning for more than a month, fond of making an extra bowl of chocolate and extra sweet bread. Who would she take her breakfast with now? When those accursed dogs barked, it would no longer be to signal the arrival of Cosi.

That night she woke again to the barking of the dogs on the neighboring roof. It must be two A.M., she thought. Who were the dogs barking at? Some passerby, sensed on the star-breeze roof of the frantic dogs. Slowly she put her feet out onto the floor and stood up, cautious as always of her stiff back. She padded through her house to the front door and unlocked the lock and pulled the door open. The dogs barked and barked, the accursed animals, one in a high voice, two others bass. In the star-shine she saw them race along the edge of the roof looking downward, and race back in the other direction to the limits of their high run. "Poor things," she thought for the first time. "They are caged on that roof. That can't be much of a life, to race along the edge of a roof and bark. That can't be much of a life even for a dog."

Then she looked across onto the cement walk that went up and down the hill, to see who was passing by. But there was nobody. She looked into the garden and saw the four-boys-in-one lying still as stone, gazing up at the stars. Slowly she closed the door and locked it and padded back to her bed. She climbed into the bed and pulled the blanket up to her ears. Still the dogs barked. Those accursed animals were barking at nothing and nobody, she knew now; there was no passerby, there was no one but a few slow stars and the rabbit in the moon, and the dogs were crazy from confinement and boredom. As she lay alone on her side of the bed her eyes filled with tears for the sad situation of the dogs.

In her next dream her four-boys-in-one were settling into the earth like stones of ten thousand years, heavy and not to be moved although outside her window the stars moved. In this dream fresh air dusted the boys with blessings. Forgotten songs tiptoed through her head while she slept.

The following morning Guendolín prepared her chocolate knowing that Cosi would not come to drink and eat sweet bread. When she finished her own, she went as usual to the front door to look at her garden, pulling her hat firmly onto her faded hair.

Her stone four-boys-in-one had settled into the soil, and hardly were visible except to the mother's eye. The unsolicited and eager blue agave, and spotted aloe, and prickly nopal, and green rose succulents appeared larger than yesterday as if it had rained overnight, although Guendolín knew it had not, because she herself had been awake to look at the stars while the dogs barked. She gazed at the street as the women going down to the market began to pass with baskets on their heads, and the students began their climb up the hill toward their school carrying mochillos full of books as heavy as stones.

Although Cosi was not present Guendolín seated herself at the small table in the patio, on the shady side of where the roof divided sun from shade. After a minute she stood and moved to the other side and sat in the sun. From either side she could discern the impression left in her garden by her stone sons, the four-boys-in-one. To herself, beneath the noise of the barking dogs, she remarked softly, "Ah."

segundo

When Segundo was ten his father left. The father went to the United States to work, and never returned. Segundo, growing up in Oaxaca with his mother and sister and brother and sister-in-law and then a niece and then a nephew, completed tenth grade. By then he was adept in the family employment. He was a weaver, like everybody in his town of Teotitlán, located half an hour's bus ride outside the city of Oaxaca, and highly recommended on all the tourist destinations. Although the town sits nicely at the foot of a mountain in a pretty area, it's known only for producing rugs. All of Segundo's life, along every street, householders opened their front rooms to show their wooden looms of all sizes and their hand-colored rugs for sale. When each tourist bus arrived the barelegged tourists, both women and men, strolled along the sidewalk and chattered like birds, but Segundo didn't know what they were saying.

When Segundo was still a child the wool for their rugs was dyed with natural dyes, made from flowers and dried insects. Segundo went with his mother to pick the flowers and then he helped her fill the big pots to boil the leaves and petals to produce the dyes.

When he grew older he could draw the weaving designs, and plan the threads of different colors. But now he was thirty, a small man with a boyish face. Most of the rugs were colored with chemical dye. Too bad, the natural ingredients grew more remote, in neighboring hills balding every year. Something in his heart shrank, but tourists didn't always know the difference, or if they did, often preferred the gaudy chemical reds and yellows. His mother frequently felt too tired to climb. If Segundo did not spend entire days from early to late searching, his mother opened the packets of chemical colors she bought in the city, and poured them like salt into the boiling water.

To make a little more money Segundo began to invite tourists into his mother's house. His mother, notified in advance, put on an embroidered indigenous dress and wrapped her head with an indigenous cloth. Segundo led the tourists into the patio and showed them the boiling pots of colors, and demonstrated how to lean over the wood fire to stir the wool. He showed them his mother's spindle, and his sister weaving. He gave them small square hand-woven coasters as gifts. His mother in her colorful dress took the tourists into their main room. It was a large rectangle with a cement floor and an altar adorned with flowers and images. From behind a crude table the mother offered soda, and home-made sweet breads. But when they departed the tourists were awkward. They didn't know if they should give the mother or Segundo money, or how to do so; and often they didn't want to buy the rugs which after all could not compete with the very best for design and weight.

When the fiestas came, for Christmas or Semana Santa, he would bring their finished rugs into the big market in Oaxaca, and set up a stall to sell them. Around him a dozen other vendors of hand-woven rugs would also find places. The tourists argued about the prices, and bought very few, because rugs are heavy to take home on an airplane. Sometimes a tourist bought a wool shoulder bag. But it hardly paid the cost of the rented stall, the bus fare and food required while his mother and he took turns sitting in the stall surrounded by rugs. At night during a week of holiday market Segundo slept on the rugs so they wouldn't be stolen. His mother took the bus back to Teotitlán and returned again in the morning.

Segundo began to think of following his father to the other side. The father wrote to his family from time to time, and wired small sums of money, from which Segundo once bought American running shoes, white with a blue zigzag. His father wrote that he worked as a gardener, and cut bushes into the shapes of animals. He sent photographs of giraffes and elephants created from green bushes, which Segundo and his family understood from other photographs they saw in magazines. The father said work paid well in California where he lived.

Segundo made inquiries. He spoke to some of the Americans residing in Oaxaca, who advised him it was dangerous to cross without documents. But Segundo couldn't afford the hundreds of pesos for tourist documents. In addition, he would have to pay a bribe to the official who issued the documents, and then buy tickets for the long bus rides. Instead, he decided to go California the way so many others did, and obtain work with his father's assistance.

He began to study English so that he would be able to find his way to his father. He studied steadily in a determined way, and made the acquaintance of Americans who offered to teach him. The first American was a man who thought Segundo was eighteen. To help the boy he gave Segundo a small job painting his house, and affectionately embraced him during the English lessons. The second American Segundo met was an elderly woman. She invited him to sit in her patio while she named various things in English, and often lectured him about the dangers of crossing the frontier. In pity she bought from Segundo one of his woven wool shoulder bags, which she admired but never used.

By now Segundo was thirty-two and had no wife, nor hope that he could afford one. His niece and nephew slept in a brick room that lacked a window. It was little more than a shed with a dirt floor, built on one side of the patio, and sometimes mice ran through. The family was in debt for the brother's wedding, because the local tradition obliges the man's family to pay for the marriage festival. The brother's festival was very large, everybody in the community contributed. One future day they would ask for a return contribution for their own festivals. It's a good system, but Segundo knew it meant that he would never be free of obligations.

Segundo could not explain his despair to the American man or to the old American woman, neither in English nor Spanish. These people each lived alone without family, on money which came from the United States. His father earned money there too. So clearly Segundo must go, or live out his life in the small rug town of Teotitlán, among the others who made rugs.

Segundo made his contact with a pollero, to get him across from Tijuana. He paid a good man, and crossed without being robbed or murdered. It was a good start.

He made his way to Los Angeles and found his father in a small house living with an American wife and three American children. His father would never return to Mexico, he was a green card worker. Segundo didn't dislike the wife, or the children who were teenagers and so sophisticated he understood nothing of what they said. He listened with them to the music they played on their stereo but he didn't know how to jump in that kind of dance. Worse, there was no work. His father apologized that at this moment the United States suffered an economic downturn, and many people who used to hire the father to cut their bushes into animals and water their flowers and lawns no longer did so.

Segundo looked around for other work. The street corners filled with other small brown-skinned Mexicans like himself, dressed in laundered jeans and wearing Mexican sombreros. Like him, they spoke a certain amount of English, carefully and slowly. Among themselves they spoke the language of their towns if they were indigenous men, or if not, they spoke Spanish. They began their wait every morning at seven o'clock in front of certain well-known stores where they could buy a coke and a cigarette or two. An American would drive up, and stop to offer them work. This work was sometimes gardening or painting or picking fruit, but while Segundo waited no automobile or truck stopped. There was no work.

The house of Segundo's father was crowded with the teenagers and music and movie magazines. Segundo didn't understand the American TV or the American food, which seemed to be mostly hamburgers covered with ketchup. His father's woman was born in the United States and although she looked Mexican, she didn't talk in Spanish or cook right. Segundo knew his father had to request that his woman permit Segundo to sleep on the living room floor. He had to ask permission of his woman, an unheard of thing. The reason was that their marriage could not be legal if the father already had a prior wife in Teotitlán. Therefore the father was not justified to hold the precious green card of a resident married to an American citizen. This came out in a strong argument after one week. The angry woman could not be placated and she shouted American words at Segundo's father.

Segundo moved to a boarding house where he shared a room with two other men. They took turns sleeping in the one bed. It was easier for the other two because they had employment and left every day. But Segundo had no employment, and when his turn came to sleep he often lay awake, staring at the odd stains on the ceiling of the yellow room. He had no money to go the movies while his roommates needed to sleep in the one bed. He was afraid to loiter too long on the street or in the park. He gave himself one more week of waiting on the corner for work. Also he would speak with others in the Mexican neighborhood. Then if no work came, he would return to

Mexico. He wouldn't even need to pay bus fare back across the border. The US government would drive him.

Some months later, Segundo was again walking on the sidewalk in Oaxaca toward the second class bus station, from a small job painting a house. Unexpectedly he met the old American woman who had advised him not to go to the United States. "But you weren't hurt!" she marveled, as if this must be the most important part of his adventure. "You weren't killed or sent to jail! Did you see your father?"

This was Segundo's own fault, that he had told this bent and wrinkled woman who wore jeans like a girl, that he had a father in California who was a gardener and who would help his son Segundo find work there.

The old woman continued gesturing and asking him questions, in the bright sun on the street.

Finally Segundo spoke. "I didn't like it there," he said. He gazed at the old American woman wearing jeans. She continued to smile and move her hands about like wind-stirred leaves. From her shoulder dangled a cloth bag of the type sewed in Guatemala.

"The food didn't suit me. It's better here." Politely he smiled. "Well then, goodbye," he said. He stepped past the woman and continued on his way.

the geranium lady

The geranium lady stood at the failing metal fence which separated her front garden from the sidewalk. Her house crouched on a steeply sloping street, and many women passed slowly on their way up toward the bus stop, or rapidly as they plunged down toward the market. Many paused at her gate to admire the green ceramic macetas filled with succulents and agave and banderas, both the red flowered and the yellow. And then their hands floated up in front of their cotton aprons as they turned to the geraniums. The geranium lady, whose name was Clara, surmised it must be an unusual flower. But so well suited, with infinite submission to the hot sun and arid air.

Like herself, she thought, a strange reassignment of her life from Canada to Mexico.

And stranger yet, to rent this little house which came equipped with bed, table, cups, plates, knives, forks and geraniums.

During the first two weeks of her residence she often opened the front door and stepped into the patio. She looked at the geraniums, all their splendid, hybrid, or muted colors jammed together beneath tall bushes. After silent contemplation she turned around and went back into the house. Really, she took no ownership of these poor plants, which she referred to as "poor" because obviously the over-crowding had left them leggy, ragged and subject to infestations of heavens knows what.

After a while she realized that despite her better judgment, she was picking off the dead flowers to encourage the new. With no conscious forethought one afternoon she had stepped off the path into the field of geraniums. Her gray hair straggled loose from its bun at the nape of her neck. Her head was unprotected from the sun. So it was a fateful day when Clara put on a sun hat before she opened her front door. From that surrender it was a short step to gloves and a hand trowel. One day she went into the town and purchased clippers.

But whose geraniums were they? The owner of her rented house shrugged. Clearly the garden had been of no concern to him for years, perhaps not since the very first tenant felt beguiled by the pos-sibilities in a patch of soil. Geraniums were available in Toronto, of course. Clara had one herself, a red one, in her sunniest window to help her through the cold months, and after Robert died the red gera-nium became the only renewed bright spot, budding in new brilliance month after month, long past the time when sympathetic friends stopped visiting.

Perhaps she recalled this when she undertook the tedious task of reviving the geraniums. The first thing was to prune the overgrown tulipán tree with its huge rose-colored flowers; and then ruthlessly trim the palm papyrus. In this climate, the geranium lady knew, killing plants was all but impossible. They simply sprouted and re-sprouted, and flung themselves into the contest for air, water and space with acrobatic turns, climbing and bending in various

directions. She began to notice butterflies, and then long-tailed doves alighted where cleaned areas revealed branches and soil. The birds twittered and bobbed, round and soft-looking in muted beige and brown, so unlike the geraniums. They fed on the loosened papyrus seeds. Perhaps, the geranium lady mused as she usually did while working in the garden, perhaps they appreciate the relief too.

For it was a relief to the present Clara, to bring order and clear space for new growth. As she cut the branches and leaves and tossed them onto the path for picking up later she almost felt the orderliness infuse her. Months of shapeless wandering aligned and joined neatly somewhere inside her, like the closing of infant bone over the fontanel. Beneath the tropical sun in her jeans and gloves and stained canvas hat she grasped the geraniums carefully but firmly.

The first time the geranium lady became aware of her audience she looked out through the metal fence. A local woman with brown skin and homemade clothing had paused. The woman smiled. The geranium lady of course smiled back. The woman said, "Very pretty, those geraniums." Although the geranium lady understood little Spanish, the sense was clear enough. She nodded, and then gestured, "Would you like some?"

The woman broke into a broader smile and nodded. Clara went inside to fetch a plastic bag, and clipped two stalks. She looked to the woman for confirmation, and the woman pointed. She wanted a coral one, and of course a white would be nice also. Among the slew of geraniums grew one Clara had not previously noticed. The color was nearly lilac, a pale purple. Not the color of geraniums at all. Clara looked at it thoughtfully.

"Very strange," she remarked to her visitor. The woman agreed, pointing and smiling. But she didn't ask for a cutting of that plant. She accepted the bag of coral and white flowers the geranium lady handed over the fence, and bent her way uphill toward the bus stop.

Clara stood quietly for a while gazing at the lilac-colored geranium before she went back into the house.

The next day another woman, this one with a young daughter, paused and smiled. Again Clara asked if her visitor would like a cutting or two, and again the offer was accepted. Clara pointed to the purple geranium and asked, "Have you seen this color geranium before?" Clearly it was a geranium. There was no mistaking the hairy leaves and acrid geranium odor. The stock looked only like the stalks of all the other geraniums growing around her feet. Her visitor seemed not to understand the question, and reluctantly Clara decided the language barrier was too great. She could not inquire about such a mystery in her limited Spanish, she didn't have the words.

The woman pointed to the colors she wanted: a red, and a red-white hybrid swirl, very pretty. The geranium lady knew her stock would not be endangered. The geraniums regenerated overnight, and although the air was very dry now in the dry season they did not cry out for water. So self-sufficient, Clara mused, as she had already forgotten their cured infestation of heaven knows what.

It became a daily event, that somebody paused at the dilapidated fence, respectfully on the sidewalk side. Clara kept a little basket of used plastic bags, ready to transmit over the top bar. Rarely she opened the gate itself; it was both heavy and subject to collapse. She kept her clippers and gloves in the same basket so that everything she required came to hand in the early morning when she stepped out to her domain. Each day she clipped dead leaves and dying flowers and waited for someone to stop. And each day someone did.

And wasn't it strange, that lilac-colored geranium. Strangeness like that held people at bay, she soon learned. Every woman admired it, but each asked for the ordinary red or pink or white.

The purple geranium grew, and the geranium lady needed to cut it, really, it needed to be cut back. But no one accepted her offer as she pointed. Nor did they accept her ultimate offer, to pass through the gate into the geranium field. She would gladly show a visitor how like the others the purple geranium was, and cut a piece to give, if only one would come closer. But the women were both shy and overly respectful.

Clara began to wish for companionship, somebody like Robert with whom she could discuss topics of the day. In Mexico naturally the topics would be very different, perhaps the garbage strike, or the new cultural center with its ancient stone artifacts cut and engraved in unimaginable ways. But she knew nobody with whom she could carry on such a conversation.

One morning while she pruned in the hot sun she stooped more closely over the purple geranium and noticed in the center of the flower an opening like a tiny mouth. The geranium had achieved long arms and a leggy appearance, sturdy and reaching out. She bent and put her ear to the little mouth, waiting. Bending for more than a few minutes ached her back. Clara wondered if she sat on the front step, a distance of a meter or so, she could hear from that position whatever the purple geranium might care to say.

The next day she went into town and bought a little bench.

The flow of passersby continued, and cut gifts were handed over the top of the fence. Now when the unknown women paused they saw her on her little bench seated in the geranium field beside the purple flowers. One day one of the women addressed Clara as Doña Geranio. Clara was wearing her favorite faded purple tee shirt and green gloves. The woman smiled as she spoke, and Clara stood with her own responding smile and went about the task of cutting. Perhaps the color of the purple flower went unnoticed among the others? The woman carried a heavy bundle, wrapped in some striped cloth, a bundle that perhaps was her sleeping child, as was common here. Clara handed the woman purple, pink and coral geranium cuttings, and tried to see if the motionless wrapped bundle on the woman's back might be a child. It was so difficult to see clearly through the fence.

The woman went on her way down the hill with her flowers

and wrapped child. Clara sat again next to the purple geranium and waited. She was so still the small soft birds settled around her, and the butterflies paused overhead. The purple geranium, strange and silent, stood gathering sun into its sturdy green stem.

The woman who accepted the purple geranium did not pass again for many days. Now when she passed by on the street she carried no bundle on her back, and her face looked to Clara like the face of a woman who grieved. Clara wanted to offer another stalk of flowers, but the woman averted her face and passed by without smiling. Clara would have spoken, but her Spanish was not sufficient, and her fear was great. Instead she returned to seat herself next to the purple colored geranium. She perched on the little bench with her knees near her bosom, and inspected the plant. The leaves remained green and upright, but thus far the plant had not put out new buds.

lidia

Lidia is skinny. She wasn't always skinny, formerly some called her a luxurious armful. But she got skinny during those months in the mental hospital when she wouldn't eat and did nothing but sob disconsolately for the lover who betrayed her. Her mother hovered anxiously, consulting with the psychologist, and bringing to Lidia's form huddled under the covers glowing dishes of gelatina, fried rolled tortillas, and fragrant casseroles of meat and carrots. Lidia presented only the blanket over her head, and her mother despaired.

But eventually such things pass, and Lidia, with the aid of Prozac and the repeated phrases her psychologist rehearsed with her, left the mental hospital. Daily she repeated to herself, "I am a worthwhile person," and "A man who betrays is not worth loving," and "Another man will come along who is ready to marry forever." More such slogans kept her going, and after a while she stopped reporting that she had glimpsed the faithless former lover passing in his car, or with another woman, or dancing at a disco.

The first year after the betrayal and Lidia's subsequent four months in a mental hospital losing weight constituted a difficult time, to say the very least. Slender Lidia, with her round face still the same roundness despite her loss of butt and breasts, went to a hairdresser and shed another pound, of hair. When her black soft curls bounced around her thin neck, her black eyes began to regain some living light. However, she had taken an oath to herself to never again climb into bed with any man before they were legally wed and committed exclusively to one another.

"Listen, Lidia," her friend Maria said, "you're only thirty-four. How can you live without sex?" And Lidia agreed it would be a torment, but the months in the mental hospital were torment worse, and she knew herself to be very frail. Maria agreed in that, at least. Lidia was less strong than a hair on her own head or a thread of pink cotton candy.

Lidia devoted herself to loving her mother and niece, and hating her sister Marta who had gained a nice husband and sweet child through recklessness and disregard for common sense. The sister Marta never suggested to her little daughter that she pick up toys from the living room they all shared, nor did the sister ever offer to wash a dish or a floor. That family lived in the house with Lidia and Lidia's mother, and when the in-laws of Marta came to visit, naturally they must be accommodated in the house also. So sometimes eight or ten people bundled into the one-bath three-bedroom house. Another portion of the house was taken over for the new computer cafe Marta had opened, with four computers neatly installed in a row, for hourly rental. Lidia, who did all the drudge work, slowly regained enough stamina and self esteem to be furious with Marta. She declared her anger to Marta, but only once. After that encounter, punctuated with loud shouting and tears, Lidia, la soltera, remained silent and swept up the child's toys without a murmur. At that time she was furious with her mother also, for failing to support her point of view, but she felt she could not complain, because after all her mother had saved her from suicide or life in a mental hospital.

And so a few years went by. Each year Lidia would wear on New Year's Eve the scarlet undergarments recommended for attracting a lover, and make the rounds of dances and fiestas hosted by her friends. Her tiny ass-less body in sleek modern polyester slacks and blouses, or party dresses she purchased with earnings from the office job she went to faithfully, was placed on display for any chance offer. But marriage first.

Weekly she and Maria would take in a movie at the Plaza, and afterward compare notes while splurging in the McDonald's next to the theater. Maria was also single, but didn't trouble herself too much with future outcomes. She paid attention to the present demands of her body, and for four years managed a sexual relationship with a married man and didn't get pregnant until the final year. It became the final year when she told her lover she was pregnant, and he said, "Adios, I'm not paying for another child, I have three at home."

Consoling the distressed and weeping Maria, Lidia cheered her on to avoid an abortion and give birth to a daughter. Lidia's reasoning was, "Well, this child will belong to you, and nobody will take her away. She'll love you until you die." Maria's mother was not happy either, but everyone knew that when a grandchild appeared the grandmother would smile despite her condemnation of yet another mouth to feed. Lidia yearned for a child of her own. But after discussing the pros and cons of having a child without a husband, Lidia decided against it. Lidia's own mother, remembering the months of the mental hospital, encouraged Lidia by saying, "You should go ahead and have a child. I won't live forever, you know." But Lidia could not go about the necessary act to obtain a child. Not without the sworn fidelity of marriage.

After their weekly movies, well into Maria's eighth month, Lidia would regale her friend with episodes from her romantic fantasies. "Rodrigo called me. He asked me to go with him to a fiesta." And the next week a downcast Lidia would report, "We danced all night but Rodrigo didn't call me again. I called him once but I will never call him again." And she didn't, and he didn't, and so another man was gone. Maria understood that Lidia lived in a repetitive pattern of hope and disappointment. There was no remedy for it, and after Maria's baby came into the world the two friends resumed going to movies dedicated to romance come true happily ever after.

Now Lidia was thirty-eight, and the time for contemplating a baby of her own was growing very short, even while Lidia's hair was again growing long, the sweet blackness of it threaded with strands of gray. The mourning period was safely behind her, but soon the breeding period would be behind her also. She sat opposite Maria at the park Sunday mornings with Maria's baby hidden under a blanket from the sun and any random brujas with an evil eye. Lidia lifted her hair and twisted it into a chignon. Maria refrained from saying, even privately to her pretty baby, that Lidia was not pretty. Her round face had looked better with short hair. Certain lines had appeared, and certain colors had faded like the men of Oaxaca who vanished across the US border like wraiths. Lidia had no objection to dating the waiters and shoe salesmen who stayed behind. She equally aspired to the doctors (like her own faithless lover) and lawyers who owned middle class accoutrements like automobiles and cell phones. But regardless of class privilege, single men played fast and loose with their sweethearts. Lidia would not accept that. Marriage or nothing.

With access to Marta's computers Lidia went on line. Sadly her attempts at contacting a date by internet yielded nothing. The respondents were too young for her, and clearly they wanted only sex. Once Lidia took the bus as far as Mexico City to meet a man. He spoke very courteously, but he was younger than Lidia and anyway not in the mood to marry. So that was the end of that. Lidia gave up using the computer for searching, and not a minute too soon, because

Marta, in her reckless way suddenly went off with her husband and child to live in Puebla where better jobs were offered, abandoning the internet rental business. Lidia missed her little niece but did less housework. Although she now felt ready and confident enough to confront Marta again with a reasoned demand for Marta's participation in the housework, Marta herself may have suspected as much —she was gone.

Lidia for a while enjoyed the peace and solitude living with her mother provided. Her mother sensibly suggested that Lidia seek a widower with a child or two, whom Lidia's mother was prepared to love as sincerely as she loved her biological grandchildren. But Lidia didn't know any widowers. A friend introduced her to one. This man ran a restaurant, and was neither too ugly nor too stupid. But Lidia felt he was not for her. Sure enough, he didn't call.

Ultimately a cousin told Lidia she was going to a party where attractive men were sure to be present, and Lidia ought to come along. Lidia, dressed in fine cherry-colored silk, went and was introduced to Jorge. It seemed like a lively beginning. Jorge liked to dance, and while not the handsomest tipo on earth, he wasn't half bad. He offered to take Lidia home, and when the taxi arrived at Lidia's door Jorge embraced her and kissed her.

The next day Lidia told Maria and everyone else she knew that she had kissed a man, and perhaps that was bad? But no one thought so; in fact even Maria, Lidia's dearest friend, believed that Lidia was acting like a fourteen year old. But hadn't Lidia always been like that: romantic and naïve? How else could she have been deceived by a man who claimed he loved her for six years and meanwhile slept with three other women? Jorge, Lidia reported with shining eyes, had noted down Lidia's phone number in a little address book. Everyone waited for Jorge to telephone and ask Lidia for a date.

Some weeks later Lidia was all too sure that Jorge would never call, but she didn't completely give up hope. She would mention Jorge from time to time to her friends, and ask if they thought he would call, and if he did, what should she say, having let him kiss her after scant hours. One chilly morning while she was riding the bus to her work she sat down next to a casual acquaintance, and in her mood of forlorn regret, mentioned the episode with Jorge. The acquaintance asked where Lidia had met Jorge, and it turned out that this was a fiesta she also had been invited to, but hadn't attended, suffering a very nasty cold at the time. But her husband had gone. And what was his name? Jorge. Lidia inquired softly what was the apellido of this Jorge, her husband. And when the woman replied, "His name is Jorge Delgado," Lidia calmly lied, "Well, the Jorge I met was Jorge Osorio. I guess there were so many people present I didn't meet them all, I'm sorry to say."

When Lidia recounted the tale to Maria, laughing somewhat hysterically, or shall we say desperately, Maria could only comment, "Good thing he didn't call you. You would have nothing to show for it, since he's married."

"Perhaps a daughter, like you have," Lidia replied sadly, although she knew well enough that without marriage nothing would come about. A kiss after all does not produce a baby. After a pause she cheered up. "On Sunday I'm going to another fiesta."

"Maybe you'll meet a nice man," Maria responded.

"Yes, of course!" Lidia agreed. "Some one who is single, and ready to marry!"

the woman next door

The woman next door was probably about her own age, fifty-something, although Barbara was cautious about counting. She lived with a sense of sixty as a distant age she hoped might be delayed indefinitely, like one of the trains here in Mexico which, despite posted schedules, never arrived. She wanted more time for the unknown pleasures a foreign country would eventually bring to her patient attention.

The woman next door strolled down the hill every day dressed in light weight slacks with a crease, and flat leather shoes, the kind Barbara herself wore in the US before Charles decided to retire to a warm climate. The neighbor's gray hair was brushed off her face in a short cut, not especially becoming. Most women in this southern state still wore their hair long, often in braids, and for certain women their hair lay like a corpse, in a shade of black which reminded Barbara of calligraphy ink. Barbara's own hair had also gone gray, and she calmly acquiesced.

She thought the neighborhood and herself were not too dissimilar.

After all, she had to talk with somebody, preferably female. The woman next door, like herself, also appeared to have an older husband who leaned on her arm. Her own husband Charles spent many hours in a chair reading, and it was only by threatening him with desertion that she moved him out of the house once daily to creep down to the zócalo, sip a chilled aguaquina, and thank god that neither of them had contracted malaria. "An ounce of prevention," Charles always said brightly, lifting his glass in salute. Barbara smiled.

Barbara finally made the acquaintance of the woman next door via the plants. The woman next door lived without pets, no dogs, or caged birds, and so did Barbara, but they both kept plants. One day when Barbara spotted her neighbor chatting at her gate with the trash collector, she gathered her own scant trash and a peso, and went out to join them. The trash collector departed pushing his barrel, and Barbara, to forestall her neighbor leaving, remarked brightly, "I love your plants!"

Thereafter, the neighbor, who identified herself as Señora Queta, and Barbara chatted frequently about the usual unusual weather, about the lack of water, and assured one another of their mutual assistance in case of emergencies. In Barbara's mind an emergency could only be something like Charles suffering a stroke, for he had a history of rich cheeses and scant exercise. She yearned to ask Señora Queta if the elderly husband she walked with daily to the market or the zócalo was also fragile, but no opportunity presented itself. They spoke only of plants. Señora Queta kept dozens of red-veined crotons in pastel buckets, pails and ceramic macetas, and they flourished, marching down the patio. Barbara herself preferred the open garden she had established with bulbous succulents and blue agave, plants of several shades of green and many convoluted forms. She liked to think she had more depth to her garden than Señora Queta exhibited in hers, more profundity.

One day the hostel on their street closed, and a black ribbon was posted above the wide locked door. Barbara approached Señora

Queta who was standing on the sidewalk chatting with her niece. Barbara knew that Señora Queta's niece was "Queta Chica", while Señora Queta was "Queta Grande". The systems of families bewildered Barbara, so she always found it safer to assume that a familial relationship existed between any two persons on speaking terms. How they paused on the sidewalk gossiping reminded her of home, a familiar neighborly pastime reminiscent of springtime and peace.

"Just for gossip!" declared Barbara, greeting the woman next door with some enthusiasm in her voice. "Do you know who died? Is the hostel for sale?" And from there they lapsed into conversation about buying houses, sharing houses, paying rents. Señora Queta's niece lived with seven other family members in a three bedroom home, and Queta Chica was hoping to move in with Queta Grande, because there was more space. Barbara felt like she could have been in America, commiserating with other women about the high cost of living. Señora Queta offered to rent Barbara and Charles another house in another colonia, but Barbara declined with a smile, "Oh, I love this neighborhood! I like my neighbors! I wouldn't want to move!" Indeed, she was comforted by seeing the same neighbors daily, although the friendship seemed never to progress. Recognizing the same market vendors and the same water vendors each day, she felt accommodated within this strange culture.

One day when Barbara was returning from the solitary evening walk she insisted on, she was passing the next door neighbor's gate when Señora Queta beckoned. "Look!" The green and yellow leaves of all her crotons hung from their stalks like rags. Their red veins had already dried.

"Whatever happened!" Barbara stared at the dead plants. It was appalling to see Señora Queta's face grim with grief and anger.

"The tortilla vendor killed them!"

For a moment Barbara was completely taken aback. Could the tortilla vendor have poured some acid or some kind of plant killer into all those pots with nobody seeing her do it?

"The evil eye," Señora Queta declared. "She killed them with her evil eye."

Barbara stepped back a pace. "Is she a witch?"

"Oh, yes, clearly!" But now Señora Queta had tilted her head and was smiling as she watched Barbara. Perhaps she mocked Barbara's effort to be politely accepting. What was the correct response? In confusion, Barbara replied, "Well, what a pity! They were so pretty." And she turned to go into her own home, pausing ever so briefly at her own garden's luxury to wonder if she should take care the next time the tortilla lady rang the bell. But what could she do? She and Charles ate few tortillas, Charles preferred bread, and she bought no more than four tortillas at a time, a paltry purchase. But she might greet the tortilla lady with more smiling concern. As she opened her front door she rehearsed another smile.

Charles was indoors as usual, in his chair, thumbing through the copy of the English language newspaper he bought, shaking his head and snorting. When she informed him of the next door plant development and the evil eye, he looked at her and guffawed. For all his age it was a brash sound that Barbara didn't really care for, but that was Charles, throwing back his head and braying, "You almost sound as if you take seriously this local nonsense!"

"Of course not," Barbara replied quietly, and she proceeded into the kitchen. She washed her hands at the sink, and then pulled from the refrigerator the vegetables for dinner. Firmly she set about the task of sorting and chopping. "Of course not," she repeated to herself. A deep pain had filled her chest, and she leaned against the kitchen counter while she worked.

The next evening Barbara strolled in another direction. The clouds of early evening were gathering the final sun, white or pink. Any moment now the temperature would fall, too, as twilight approached. She sat down on the stone wall in front of the grand church where the tourists passed by in an anonymous stream of shopping bags, sundresses and floppy hats. She watched them knowing what they had bought for their families at home, the blouses and the carved wooden figures. This scene, like seasons, never changed. They were standard, both the tourists and the tourist gifts.

She sat, gazing about the plaza. A young girl in a shabby skirt approached. "Buy these flowers!"

"No, thank you."

"They are only ten pesos, buy them!"

"No. No. No, thank you!" The fuchsia flowers were small, and didn't look very fresh.

"Only ten pesos!" Then the girl was peering into Barbara's face. "But why are you crying?"

"Ah," Barbara replied. "I am crying because I have no coin for buying flowers."

The girl turned away. Barbara sat in the fading light.

claudia's world

There's no spring in Oaxaca. The bougainvillea and trumpet flowers bloom twelve months, wet season and dry. It's raining now, a daily event at five o'clock when winds picks up and water pours down. Thunder and lightning vibrate. The shifting air descends fresh and cool, it brings that smell of dampened dust I have always loved.

My student Claudia arrived for her English lesson; she trotted into the patio late at four-fifteen, wearing her blue nylon athletic jacket and pants. I am preparing to leave Oaxaca and must have looked a bit preoccupied. Claudia asked me if Robert, who's here another two months, could manage without me, and of course he can. Not so her husband, who is old-style macho Mexican. Claudia says these men have heavy balls: they can't get up off the chair to serve themselves. If she leaves for even a day she has to arrange for a replacement to cook and wash up after him.

The women of Tehuantepec on the Isthmus of Oaxaca are raised differently, she informs me. They rule. Claudia leans her elbow on the patio table; she makes a fist and flexes her biceps. The women rule. They rule in the markets and streets as vendors; all the family income derives from their efforts and enters their hands. Claudia says they drop toloache into their husbands' tea, day by day, poisoning the men slowly, so the men become idiots.

Claudia was Tehuantepec-born, and it's clear to see she wishes she lived there now. Her husband is more than twenty years her senior; she married a middle-aged divorced doctor when she was a nineteen year-old nurse. Then, it was a good deal. The doctor was respected, and although doctors make no more than middle-class money in Mexico, still he was respected. He elevated Claudia over a life of vending tamales and fish. But the aging doctor Romulo naps every afternoon; he doesn't want to travel or dance or go to clubs and movies, and he won't let her go. She lies. And sex is disappearing. Her gynecologist told her the reason she has inflamed ovaries is because of insufficient sex. I think he was imagining a curative proposal.

I've told her Robert can cook, do laundry and clean, and he does. She told me her son can, too. He's eighteen. The doctor father says young Emilio has intelligence, but although Claudia thinks Emilio is actually brilliant, she knows it has more to do with modern culture than intelligence. The culture on the Isthmus has always been different.

I admire Claudia's biceps; she plays tennis and thinks nothing of swimming 70 laps. She's very athletic, although God knows that's no substitute for sex. She has considered toloache. She says she'd rather have a husband with heavy balls than an idiot. Her husband the doctor Romulo speaks a kind of English. He tells me he's very interested in homeopathy, so maybe he's an idiot after all. But a generous one, who holds free clinic hours for poor people, although

officially he's retired. He looked at my skin for me, and recommended a specialist. The specialist told me I need a stronger sun block, but still I thought Romulo acted very kindly. He's a non-stop talker. If I were Claudia I might try toloache to shut him up. Emilio is learning English too; he's planning to go to law school because there aren't too many professions offered in Oaxaca and few in Mexico where people find employment—not much going on for architects, engineers or chemists. Claudia herself wanted to become a doctor, but for a poor woman that wasn't possible. She did well to become a nurse. Claudia's not thrilled by a law career for her brilliant son, but let him choose. Romulo studied medicine in the USA. The former president of Mexico, Lopez Portillo, is on his way to Houston for a heart by-pass.

Lopez Portillo's wife appeared breathless with anxiety, on television. She's an aged beauty, with something on her skin that appears very strange on the screen, some sort of plastic mask or maybe cosmetic surgery, done in Houston. She displays good bones, though; thank god bones hold up when all else goes.

Claudia's skin sun-weathered from her athletic life, but she's only forty-five, with this garrulous old retired doctor husband who's devoted to homeopathy. He naps each afternoon and won't stand up to put his cold coffee into the microwave. He won't clear off the table after he eats. But he drives his car, and Claudia owns a car too. They both drive to the "country club" to play tennis. Claudia competes in an annual tournament, and this year she's going to win because she never gets laid and she never gets to travel on vacation.

Everyone seems to know a matriarchy rules the Isthmus. The women count the money as it enters the door in the hands of their children. The women strut tall and handsome, often larger than the men, but in fact I never see Istmenian men in the city of Oaxaca. Not that they don't come, but they don't come in identifiable costume. They look just like everyone else in their poor gabardine pants or jeans, demanding the government remedy this or that.

The women, however, act haughty. They use their income, Claudia says, to put on gold: gold necklaces, gold bracelets, gold earrings, gold teeth. They wear waist-length embroidered blouses and ankle-length full skirts over petticoats. They frequently march on little black shoes in parades, the ones who live here in the city and those up visiting from the coast; in these parades they carry organization banners and standards like sororities, they carry flowers on their shoulders. Each wears her black hair braided with ribbons and wound in a wreath, or maybe she covers her head with a white lace starched headdress. Claudia says she owns her costume, too. Although I've never seen her in it, I notice the gold hoops in her ears when she returns from playing tennis.

Claudia's first language is Zapotec. Her French immigrant grandfather married a woman of Tehuantepec. Claudia learned Spanish when she started to school, and I guess her mother did too. Government data declare the population of the state of Oaxaca as 60% indigenous, but it puzzles me as to who's who. And who wins in the indigenous game. Claudia's not indigenous. Arturo and Oskar, whose families are pure Zapoteco, are not indigenous. Manuel is not indigenous, although his family is Zapoteco also. Venancio who speaks Mixe is not indigenous, he's a cop. They're all Mexican, and Oaxacan, except for Claudia who identifies herself as an Istmenian. From Tehuantepec.

When we talk about the Zapatistas Claudia displays enormous sympathy. Because they're so poor. Her own mother was poor, her father died when she was young and there were five children or maybe six, I forget. The women are vendors, not producers. Now Claudia is the only one of her siblings who has sufficient means to provide food and clothing for the mother. The mother lives in Tehuantepec but comes to visit, not too often since naturally some antipathy lurks between her and a man her own age with heavy testicles. But Romulo the doctor gets even, by being a doctor. He can tell Claudia's mother that she suffers irregular heartbeats, or skin cancer. He shows his mother-in-law his advantage, they reach an equilibrium. No toloache for the doctor. Claudia loves her mother more than she loves Romulo, I think, but it's Romulo's money that keeps her mother fed. Nothing is simple.

Claudia tells me the Tehuantepec women learn to sell tamales or whatever produce their mothers hand them, from a very young age. They walk door to door carrying tamales, like girls do here in the city of Oaxaca. We buy from a hot bucket, outside our gate on Sunday mornings at 8:00. Three kinds: sweet, chicken with mole, chicken with roja. But the girl who sells them is probably already twelve or thirteen. The street kids (and are they indigenous?) here, as in Chiapas, start at age five or six selling Chiclets, polishing shoes and begging.

On Friday, April 27, 2001 the Mexican congress passed into law an amended and false version of the so-called Law of COCOPA, the San Andrés Accords. It gives indigenous towns the right to autonomy, the right to associate themselves into municipalities, the right to operate their own means of communication, the right to bilingual education, and it prohibits slavery. It declares that discrimination is forbidden.

It permits individual states to see to all that.

It says translation will be offered where needed, so no denial of health and education services will occur. It defines the obligations of the nation in matters of economic and social development. It guarantees collective use and enjoyment of lands and resources. The use and disposition of the natural resources by indigenous people are called "preferential". The supreme law of the land is Mexico's constitution.

> *The Mexican nation is multicultural, founded originally in its indigenous peoples, who are those descended from populations who inhabited the present-day territory at the time of [Spanish] colonization and who have kept their own social, economic, cultural and political institutions, or portions of them.*

> *The Mexican Nation is one and indivisible.*

Claudia tells me what I already know, about parents in autonomous indigenous communities selling their daughters in marriage regardless of the girls' wishes. We also know that the Zapatista army attracted more than half women soldiers; fighting was one of their better options. And a woman, Esther, gave the first speech in front of Congress when the Zapatistas went to plead for the Accords. In the newly passed Constitutional law, women are guaranteed equal rights with men.

And here comes the response to the law: the EZLN is pissed. Pablo Salazar, governor of Chiapas, doesn't care for it. Luis Alvarez, the COCOPA liaison, pleads for acceptance and more negotiation later on. The current bishop of Chiapas, Arizmendi, asks for acceptance, like it's God's will.

Women will have equal rights.

AAs Pablo Salazar points out in response to the Zapatistas' rejection of the new law: The country has changed. The conditions for the peace process have also changed. What hasn't changed is a mentality that remains clad in prejudices and unfounded fears... it keeps the people as objects of public interest and doesn't recognize them as they demand to be: actors in the public realm... If the [indigenous] peoples remain objects of interest, they are limited to being recipients of public policy; if they achieve the status of subjects by right, their towns and communities will participate in organization of the State. The absence of the right to participation and to become protagonists in the construction of their present and future is what causes them to reject the approved law of rights and indigenous culture.

Like thanks, but no thanks. I know why Claudia tells me about toloache. I know why nobody around here is indigenous. The sticking point on the new law is not men with heavy balls sitting on their latifundias while others pick their coffee. No; the issues are ownership, control, participation and paternalism. No matter how kind or generous old Romulo may be, Claudia thinks about what to put in his tea.

the high fence

The American woman had a fence in front of her house, but there's no fence that keeps out a cat, and furthermore this fence was made of the thinnest, cheapest metal wire, and stood not very high. It wouldn't keep out a thief, let alone a cat, the American woman grumbled to herself.

The cat used the tiny garden of the American woman as a toilet. It was a male cat, and in the fresh morning air when the American woman stepped outside to greet the day, the odor of cat piss greeted her first.

The American woman was not disliked by her neighbors who regarded her as a curiosity, an unlikely creature with short frizzy bronze hair and bare feet in sandals although Americans can afford shoes. The neighbors greeted her and she greeted them; it was an amiable street with several stuccoed adobe and cement houses painted blue, yellow and red.

Therefore it was easy enough one morning when a neighbor passed on the way to market, for the American woman to ask, "Please, can you tell me where it's possible to purchase cat repellant?"

The neighbor, a plump old woman who limped on the arm of her granddaughter, waited politely while the American woman found the appropriate Spanish words, "There's a male cat who is using my garden for its personal needs."

Repellant? The neighbor replied there was no such product for sale in this small city. They all thought of themselves as poor Mexicans because if they weren't poor at the moment they might be tomorrow. The granddaughter stared at the American woman incredulously and kept silent. The old neighbor suggested to the American woman perhaps she could put out poison. The neighbor smiled politely and continued on her way to the market.

The American woman was appalled. Poison a cat! Certainly not! But the old neighbor appeared so amiable and sincere.

The next day when the cat clearly was persisting in its nasty habit, the American woman went to the gate in her usual jeans, tee-shirt and sandals. She asked again of her neighbor, "But who owns this cat?" The elderly neighbor, nicely dressed in a matching polyester yellow vest and skirt, and wearing sturdy leather shoes, leaned on her granddaughter and replied the cat was homeless of course; nobody would mind if it were poisoned. But the American woman widened her mouth in distress.

This American woman was middle-class by birth, and a university graduate like her parents and siblings. She earned her income by writing for elite English journals and magazines her analyses of cultural and social currents, often accompanied by not strictly academic witty commentary. Recently, she had decided to go to Mexico for warmth and serenity and to write her first novel, her first attempt at fiction. It was going well until the cat appeared, because the American woman's schedule embraced a healthy and peaceful alternation of outdoor work in the garden and sitting at her computer. In the evenings she often strolled to the center of town to see whatever outdoor performance of music or dance was offered for tourists.

Her routine was pleasant, and the cat presented an annoyance.

Again the following day she stopped her neighbor who by now was becoming accustomed to pausing in the street to discuss the cat piss problem. The granddaughter had not yet spoken. When the American woman again asked if there were nothing to buy, the old woman and the granddaughter both thought hard. Finally the elderly neighbor suggested that the American woman go to the chemist's shop and inquire if there were some product. If not, the granddaughter finally suggested, that was also the place to purchase poison. The American woman could see in their eyes, however polite, that the notion of paying money for cat repellant advertised a peculiar foreign indulgence.

Nevertheless she took her shoulder bag and set out for the ferretería in the center of town, and pursuing three wrong instructions, she finally located it on a dusty side street among other shops. Inside, she asked for cat repellant and was answered with only a smile and raised eyebrows. To her disappointed expression the small man behind the counter offered, But we have poison. And when the American woman shook her head, he advised her to try at the veterinarian pharmacy. By the end of the day the American woman had tried the ferretería, the pharmacy, the veterinarian, and a nursery that sold plants. Clearly her only recourse was to order by internet a cat repellant to be sent to Mexico by special delivery.

The American woman calmed herself. A high burst of laughter at her own notion indicated stress. She sat down. She recognized the absurdity of her problem. Nevertheless she would not have that horrible odor greeting her every morning, to say nothing of the damage to her well-tended plants. Therefore another plan must be devised, and no, she was not going to murder this cat. In her heart she deeply hoped that one of the neighbors would murder it, so she would have nothing on her conscience, and a clean garden. But meanwhile something must be done.

In the middle of the night the American woman woke from her sleep with an idea. This was common for her, because she was a writer and often received themes and solutions in the middle of the night; not dreamed exactly, but worked out by her subconscious. She came to Mexico for her subconscious to function undistracted by the noise and misery of New York, and when this very subconscious dutifully coughed up a solution, it was not to be disregarded. So what idea for the cat? Ah, find a local bruja, a witch who would have all sorts of herbal and non-toxic solutions to the cat piss problem. Satisfied with this line of thinking she turned over and went back to sleep.

In the morning she wondered how she was going to locate a witch or an herbalist, whatever. Perhaps best begin at the local market, where she could ask for a remedy; and so the American woman cast about for suitable language to inquire for an herbalist or a witch who knew cures for ailments such as cat improprieties. She wanted words for the remedy which would be sufficiently explicit to get results, but not culturally offensive. She drank her coffee and considered with her dictionary open on the table. Maybe she should ask for someone who knew how to drive away unwanted guests. That might do. It certainly described the cat. And if she found a witch who was recommended along those lines, she definitely was on the right track.

Thus determined, the American woman put on her sun-glasses, lay her straw hat atop her bronze hair, took up her shoulder bag again and checked for keys, handkerchief and wallet. She opened the door and stepped into the horrible odor left by her unwanted guest.

In the market she found a small stall set up with various powdered spices and herbs in plastic bags tied with pieces of dry vine, and labeled in Spanish. It looked promising. But to her query about driving away unwanted guests the woman tending the stall replied, "Why don't you turn up the TV real loud with Big Brother on it?" The woman herself was watching a tiny portable TV wired to an invisible outlet.

The American woman felt deeply distressed. What kind of country had she come to, anyway? Where was the magic, the culture, the profundity that nourished her midnight waking, and permitted her to write thousands of words about the subtleties of cultures less crass than her own?

"What I mean," she explained with her eyes downcast, "is some powder to drive away a cat who is using my garden for its personal needs."

"Well!" the stall woman exclaimed. Clearly she thought the American woman the most foreign of foreigners, bordering on the incomprehensible. "Why don't you poison it? It must be homeless."

The American woman shook her head. She didn't bother to explain she was not capable of poisoning a cat, and especially not if the cat might take a convulsion and die right there among the opuntia and crassulacea. The cat must be convinced that it's true home was elsewhere.

As the American woman continued in her walk about the market for other errands, it crossed her mind that the solution might be worse than she had thought. For instance, she might drive away the cat by covering all the available soil with razor wire, but then she herself would be driven away. Likewise if she used only beer cans cut in strips, or broken glass. The cat would be unable to scratch and she would be unable to kneel among her plants, unable to tend them and pick off the faded yellow leaves, a caretaking gesture that reminded her of a boyfriend of long ago who used to ask her to squeeze the pimples on his back. At signs of her mother's disapproval she had broken off that relationship soon thereafter, and never saw the boy again, but perhaps that was her first experience of intimacy with another living creature, that grooming. She often saw couples who appeared to groom or feed one another, and the American woman wondered if she were somehow defective because the best she could do was write descriptions and assessments of other people's lives, while she herself scarcely had one. Grooming the garden made her think better of herself. After all, plants are living creatures.

Logically, the next day she put out a bowl of milk for the offensive cat, and waited for him to come and enjoy it. Which he did not, although the following morning the milk was gone, and the odor was refreshed. So she was wooing a cat. Now truly the next step was to abandon all the plants in favor of care-giving and perhaps eventually grooming this higher life-form, and she let the garden run wild, since in Mexico plants seemed to never die but only transform themselves, as if they contained their own witches. She became intent on creating a perfect cat haven. She began to place outside her door fish heads and meat scraps, until finally one day the cat, a gray striped creature with a fat tail, came to eat in her presence. So she had accomplished her goal.

But wait a minute, what was her goal? Certainly originally her goal was to enjoy her garden and create her novel. Both those ideas had gone astray. She had slipped into self-improvement, an often pointless task. Certainly she hadn't intended to really change herself into an animal lover, so drastic! Now she was surrounded by foul-smelling garbage, cat piss odors, and worst of all, in all this care-giving and generous love for a homeless creature, she had stopped writing. Was that true? Yes, she could see on her laptop that the kilobytes had increased by only 197 in two weeks! Two weeks with nothing written! If her livelihood were at stake she'd do better to murder the cat.

Now the American woman felt totally confounded. She stopped feeding the cat, which nevertheless came to her door and cried, and then at night relentlessly soiled her now wild garden. So she had neither an object of her human affection nor an odor-free breath of air.

As always she turned again to logic and American common sense. She decided to simply abandon her little house and find another elsewhere, cat free. This she set about doing with great reluctance because she enjoyed her little house where until recently the writing had gone well, and the garden until recently had grown to her bidding, and the neighbors until recently had regarded her with pleasant disinterest. All gone, all lost to this wretched cat.

Well, life must go on.

She found another small house on another pleasant street, on the other side of the small city zócalo. The new house was behind a high stucco wall painted yellow, and the garden lay in the rear. It was not until she had paid for the first two months and moved her computer and clothing, that she realized the high wall in front discouraged the pleasantries she'd enjoyed among her previous neighbors, and the rear garden was accessible to any cat, by way of the adjacent roof.

Both these circumstances she shut out of her mind, intent on completing the first draft of her book, come what may. As she came and went through the gate in her high wall for her usual marketing and post office errands, she pretended she had many friends elsewhere, and no time to smile or chat. When she sat alone in her garden behind her small house she felt no interest in gardening, and let the flowers and vines range freely like chickens of prior times. Nevertheless the writing was not going well. As she re-read her chapters she saw a dreadful sense of futility had crept into her tone. The characters supposed to enjoy life were desperately unhappy, and those invented to be desperately unhappy seemed to not give a damn. It was a trick of poor word choice, she supposed, or whatever. But there it was.

In sorrow she decided she must kill the novel in its youth and begin again. Killing the novel proved to be easier than killing a cat only in that no blood was evident, nor sullied fur and dry teeth. But she herself in her own foreign way suffered by fiction-proxy the murder of a living thing. She had become more fond of the characters she had created than of any well-groomed boyfriend.

However, she was determined to begin again and get it right. Her first chapters went well, and she monitored carefully the sense of mood created by her phrases: long, short, lilting, stifled, profound and silly. But at the fifteenth chapter she again felt it was going badly, and stopped writing. Instead, she spent more evenings at the tourist attractions, watching the costumed dancers in their repetitive motions, listening to dreadful renditions of "Granada" played by a wobbly solo trumpet, and attending lectures in Spanish where she understood very little. Her life started to imitate the futility she had expressed.

She began to suppose the warmth and ease of Mexico were ruining her personality. Very likely New York, despite harsh winter days when she never went out, and hot stifling summer nights on the street when sleepless neighbors gathered to play music and drink cold beer, New York held her true soul. Her home was there, with her subconscious. Reluctantly, she suspected that fiction was not her genre, and the elitist essays at which she had become so proficient better suited her abilities. She could explain cultures not only of Mexico and Guatemala but of Indonesia and Madagascar where she'd never been. She could outline the changes that were taking place as the world pounced upon local societies, sowing American music and jeans. It was what she was best at.

Sadly, but with American determination, she gathered her belongings and bought her plane ticket to Mexico City and her plane ticket to New York. She packed some of her books and gave the rest to indifferent second-hand book vendors. She locked her computer into its black nylon case and handed her door-key over to her landlord. She had arranged for a taxi to come on the correct day and drive her to the airport. Things just hadn't worked out.

In the taxi en route to the airport she gazed from the window with stifled regret. Along the road she saw for the last time the Mexican people on their normal tasks; the horrible traffic, the almost colliding buses, the frenzy of flowers on unruly bushes. And then she spotted a dead cat by the side of the road, already flattened and dried, clearly done in by the wheels of some vehicle. The cat had no time as her taxi rushed past, to greet the American woman. Nor was she sure if the cat was her cat. In any case, it no longer would soil anybody's garden. Briefly the lips of the American woman turned up with satisfaction. Justice prevailed.

messages in a small town

Jorge was seated at a table in a corner of the restaurant at 3:00 o'clock in the afternoon, the hour for la comida. The restaurant was filling slowly, with business men wearing neat cotton shirts and a couple with their baby and grandmother. As was often the case, there were more waiters than patrons. They attended him carefully.

His heart thumped happily to the sounds of dishes tapped with knives and forks, and the casual chatter of waiters. The restaurant provided him with the sense that he and Socorro were embraced by the people of the town, although this was an illusion. The reality was that Jorge was eating la comida with his cell phone. Socorro, a kilometer away in her home with her husband, made the plan. They would connect. Socorro would leave her cell phone open in the kitchen, and each time she moved from the dining room to the kitchen they could exchange a few words. Her husband need never know.

The husband was of the old school, macho. Socorro, snuggled in the arms of Jorge those few evenings when the husband Rodolfo visited his mother, often referred to her husband as a man with heavy huevos. This meant he couldn't get up from his chair, not to bring himself a cup of coffee, or to return a plate to the kitchen. He must be waited on hand and foot.

Rodolfo was older than Socorro by twenty-five years, and this circumstance provided her with a comfortable way of life. She made frequent trips to Puebla to fetch packages for Rodolfo, and sometimes drove to Mexico City to buy the latest fashion in pants suits and high heeled sandals. She went by herself if she could, in the yellow VW bug Rodolfo presented her with on her fortieth birthday. On those occasions Jorge met her in the large anonymous city, and they would enjoy a few hours in a hotel room. Afterward, Socorro and Jorge went together to a department store where Socorro completed hasty purchases with Jorge's approval of color and style, and then she sped to the large pharmacy where the insulin for Rodolfo waited.

Usually Socorro spent most of her day directing the muchacha in cleaning and laundering, and shopping for fruit and vegetables at the local market. Although Rodolfo could easily afford a grand modern refrigerator, he insisted those machines were too pretentious, and like everyone else he would have a small refrigerator or none, and buy fresh food daily. By that he meant that Socorro would buy fresh food daily, taking with her the muchacha who carried the provisions in a red woven plastic shopping bag with white plastic handles, exactly like those everyone else carried.

Socorro personally selected the meats, because Rodolfo, lean as a papyrus stalk, insisted on eating meat three times daily. He also managed his diabetes with cereal and honey, and although sixty-five might not be considered elderly for country people who worked in the fields until they died at eighty, Rodolfo often behaved as if his days ahead were few. If no business was at hand he spent long afternoon hours on the sofa dozing, or remembering his youth. Sometimes his still-hovering mother telephoned, and then Socorro would hear Rodolfo recite in a languid way names of the dead, dozens of dead: aunts, cousins, grandparents, friends, all the extended relationships.

He even knew which of his tocayos, men with his same given name of Rodolfo, had died. Rodolfo García suffered a stomach cancer and his cousin Rodolfo García Laro died in a terrible highway accident.

When Socorro and the muchacha arrived back at the house from the market the muchacha set the foods to soak in iodine to kill the parasites. By then it was the hour to cook comida, and sit opposite Rodolfo while he cut his meat into tiny pieces and extended his pinkie finger as he held his rolled tortilla. With this routine she often felt desperate, desperate with boredom from her life with Rodolfo. Hence the idea for the cell phone comida together with Jorge.

Socorro broached the idea to Jorge one afternoon when Socorro went to the pharmacy to order insulin to be delivered to Puebla. She could easily chat in her VW, and she even sat on a bench in the park; everyone used cell phones these days. Jorge was at his office in the green and yellow government building a block away, scheduling hearings for people who sought appointments with the mayor. He pushed aside the calendar and names of townspeople, and put down his pencil to answer his cell phone. When he heard Socorro's voice he made little kisses, and at the other end of the satellite connection arcing over their part of the globe, she did the same. These kisses made it possible for Jorge to work in a kindly way, estimating the need of the people who petitioned.

Socorro felt pleased with her comida idea, and it was the task of Jorge to mention every conceivable mishap. If Rodolfo found out about their affair, things would go badly all around, because Rodolfo ran the only cash income business for the town, which was transporting marijuana. The entire town depended on his expertise, knowing when and whom to bribe, his business acumen. If Rodolfo discovered his wife's infidelity who knows what steps he might take. No doubt the entire town would suffer, and this sense of public responsibility weighed on Jorge, who had assumed a serious air when he became a public official.

Socorro assured him that even if Rodolfo found the cell phone he would not know it was connected up in the sky to the lover of Socorro. It was quite dubious that Rodolfo would even stand up during comida! All she need do was maintain her kitchen trips to bring each course in its regular sequence: the soup (trip to kitchen), the rice (trip to kitchen), the meat (trip to kitchen), the desert (trip to kitchen). And then of course she could go fetch the jar of cold fruit drink, or coffee if Rodolfo asked for coffee. The muchacha, finished with her shopping and laundry chores, stayed out in the patio eating her own food by herself at a small table sheltered beneath the eaves. When she finished eating and came to wash the dishes, Socorro must disconnect the cell phone. How simple.

Therefore Jorge took himself to the restaurant during the dinner hour at 3:00 o'clock so they could dine together, he and Socorro. He held the tiny telephone in one hand in order to drink, or occasionally he tucked it under his chin so he could easily cut his food to eat. As he put each mouthful between his lips he tried to form the exact phrase to convey his sensations, so that when Socorro returned to the connection he could tell them to her. She explained to Jorge her sensations also, which were not always about the food but about her husband's diminished sex drive, her longing for the arms of Jorge, and her miserable life as the financially comfortable wife of the sole transporter of marijuana in this isolated mountain town.

This comida togetherness continued for more than a week. Day of the Dead was approaching, the harvest at the end of the rainy season, November First. The marijuana transport was heavier than usual, a fine crop coming in from the hills around them. Rodolfo had his hands full hiring boys to dry the baskets of leaves and little purple buds, to seal kilo bundles wrapped in plastic, and place them snugly within big sacks surrounded by rich-smelling compost, as if they were carrying only compost, to the grand hacienda where the marijuana would be received, weighed, and sent on its way. Rodolfo was occupied rounding up trucks and drivers, paying the appropriate officials on the roads, then paying the drivers with cash advance against the safe delivery, and assuring them that failure to return would be dangerous for the entire town which depended on their honesty.

The following week on Wednesday, after enjoying several happy meals with Jorge by telephone, Socorro returned to the dining room carrying their plates of rice. Rodolfo sat with his face pale and trembling. He looked ill, and Socorro wondered if his blood sugar had fallen. She looked at him anxiously, because as a good Catholic she might wish him to die but only in God's good time and by God's decision.

"Do you hear the voice?" Rodolfo asked her in a whisper.

"What voice!"

"I believe the angel of God is speaking to me. I hear a voice in the other room when you leave."

Socorro looked at Rodolfo with terror. Finally she managed, "Why would the angel of God speak to you?"

"I don't know! How could I know! I'm a humble man and have always gone to church and showed kindness to others. This entire town sleeps under my wing. I don't have any dealings with God; God stays in the church where he belongs and I am in the town where I belong! I understand nothing of this!" Rodolfo took his napkin and wiped the sweat from his face. Socorro made a mental note to ask the muchacha to wash the napkin.

Rodolfo said nothing further about hearing a voice in the distance. Socorro breathed a sigh of relief, and the next day did not call Jorge, who sat in the restaurant surrounded by obsequious waiters, waiting for her ring until it was altogether clear that today there would be no happiness. He paid his bill and left, wondering.

The following day, however, which was Friday, Jorge went again to the restaurant. This time Socorro, breathless and in a frightened whisper, told Jorge that Rodolfo had received a visitation. For several days now, he heard the voice of an angel speaking to him. They both knew he could not hear Socorro during comida, not possibly, through the heavy swinging door to the kitchen. Therefore it must be an angel, or a spirit.

Socorro told Jorge to stop going to the restaurant, and wait prepared to hear further news. She returned to the dining room, where Rodolfo still sat in his heavy chair. He was smiling. He greeted the plate of fried meat with a nod, and said, "This angel, or maybe it's a visitation from the Virgin, who knows. This voice addressed me very clearly. She told me to wait."

"Wait for what?" Socorro could hardly speak from fear. Her voice lodged in her throat like a bite of dry tortilla. To clear the way for her words she sipped from her glass of watermelon juice and repeated, "Wait for what?" The townspeople awaited the Day of the Dead, which would be widely celebrated, and many households had already adorned altars with fruits, squash and special breads. The orange chrysanthemums gave off a heavy aroma which made Socorro sneeze. In their home Rodolfo each year asserted that Día de los Muertos was a superstitious practice, a cult that believed the dead would visit, and he himself was a modern man. So they neglected preparations for the day, although of course in the town they were courteous and understanding of their fellow citizens.

"I don't know. She didn't say. But how else am I to wait? I go to confession and I visit my mother. What more must I do?"

The marijuana truck rumbled safely on its way, and Rodolfo via his cell phone was informed of its arrival at the hacienda. He had only to expect the money to come back with the drivers, and then distribute the income to those who worked for it: growing, cutting, packing and shipping, keeping for himself only the amount due him to cover expenses and provide Socorro with nice clothes. He was satisfied, except for that voice, which now plagued him in the deepest hours of the night.

At first he imagined somebody was in the patio, or worse, in the garage with their two VW Bugs. But the dogs did not bark, and the chilly night remained quiet. Only the voice, a soft feminine trill, continued. But he could not make out the words. Of course he waited, well prepared for anything! Day of the Dead approached, and if he had been wrong all these years, and the dead did return, which of his dead could it be? Or the Virgin? Or a messenger? Rodolfo tried to remain calm. Death was not the worst event; he had enjoyed a full life with his first wife before he found Socorro. If his own time to die had come, he could leave knowing that his work on behalf of his town had been most beneficial. Someone would succeed him. But who? Ah, that was a puzzle. It was needful that his successor be a younger man, but one mature and sensible enough to deal calmly with the armed officials and unofficials of the highway and of the federal government, all of whom expected their complicity to be well rewarded. The town must rely on a man with a keen sense of what was just.

Rodolfo returned to his bed and lay down beside Socorro, who snored gently. His young wife fortunately never bore children, a blessing from God because Rodolfo fathered twelve in his first marriage bed and who knows how many others. He had fulfilled his duty to be fruitful and multiply. Socorro had not, but this was not his fault, nor could he remedy the situation. So he stroked his wife's sleeping form and settled on the pillow to think.

Yes, a successor would be necessary, one whom Rodolfo could invest, with a calm sense of having done his final duty. He stroked his wife, and she shifted in her sleep and whispered to him, "Jorge".

Diós mío! The town had several men named Jorge, who did she mean? How had she read his thoughts even from within her deep sleep, his dear wife who tended him so well, not permitting him even to rise from the table to bring his own coffee or return his own plate to the kitchen! Who went so faithfully to the pharmacy to make sure his insulin was ordered, and drove to Puebla when it was necessary to bring the precious package back. His treasure, the lovely Socorro, from within a dream responded to his question! Turning over in his mind the several men he knew named Jorge, he waited fretfully until morning when Socorro woke.

"And who is this Jorge?" He tried to remain calm, but a sleepless night had done him no good. His face looked anxious, and his eyebrows went wild above his eyes, turning in every direction like gray wires.

Socorro gasped. So after all he knew! And she could do nothing but confess and plead with him not to kill her. She hesitated. Surely she should not reveal the name of her lover, that would lead only to worse confrontations. "And who is this Jorge?" Rodolfo asked again. He took her by the shoulder and turned her toward him, embracing her. Socorro, near to fainting, whispered, "Jorge Quesada Luna, who works in the mayor's office."

"Ah," Rodolfo sighed. Again he lovingly embraced his wife, and went to the dining room to enjoy his morning coffee, eggs and sausage. Socorro observed his peaceful face and trembled.

The funeral took place on November third, the final observed day of Days of the Dead. Rodolfo had died peacefully in his chair after dinner, gazing at his dear wife with a smile of satisfaction, knowing he had arranged all satisfactorily. At the cemetery the entire town was present. Since most people yearly without fail attended family Day of the Dead observations, music and food were abundant inside and in the puestos beyond the gates, and much mescal flowed at a polite distance from the new grave. Socorro wore an elegant black pants suit and black high heeled sandals. She seemed to tremble now and then, as if some grief or strayed angel passed over her.

Jorge also attended the funeral ceremony, bowing his head and closing his eyes. Humbly he prayed that he would take Rodolfo's place in such a way as to bring satisfaction to everyone.

sleeping beauty

Few people in rural Mexico know the story of Sleeping Beauty, which after all is a European tale, and furthermore involves a wicked step-mother, a creature nearly unheard of in this part of the world where each baby belongs to one or two parents, grandparents, cousins, aunts, and uncles, plus a godmother and godfather in reserve against evil events.

Nevertheless, the tale was known to Homero, who had studied literature at the University in Mexico City, and at the age of thirty read myths and legends in English, French and German, in addition to his native Spanish.

Moreover, as a Mexican must, he knew the story of the Sleeping Virgin, a girl who at age fourteen had fallen into a coma, but due to constant prayers by her aunt, had not died.

Now, one might think this aunt wicked as a wicked step-mother, because as years went by she erected a shrine in her interior patio, and on Sundays permitted the reverent and docile to pass through. They tiptoed up to the raised bed, and peered through the mosquito canopy to see the smooth expressionless face and the folded hands intertwined with a rosary displayed on the outer coverlet. Winter and summer are much the same in this part of the world, and the aunt had devised the simple expedient of keeping the girl outside so as to minimize odors and also lend to the sight an aura of genuine beauty, provided by constantly blossoming bright flowers with occasional hummingbirds and doves. As the reverent and docile passed by the virgin's bier they genuflected, crossed their torsos and kissed their thumbs. If they chose, they could purchase for two pesos a white lily dusted with holy breezes from the patio. If they chose only to gaze and pass, the fee nevertheless was two pesos, which the aunt used to maintain the shrine of her sleeping niece.

Of course under such circumstances it was necessary to maintain in attractive order the house through which the visitors passed in a line that often was so long the devout waited inside the living room for an hour, gazing at the pictures of Jesus, Mary and the Saints displayed on the walls, before passing out to the virgin's garden. It was also necessary that the aunt be dressed attractively, and her hair be nicely coiffed. Custom and culture would not permit otherwise, this Homero knew as well as anyone. He begrudged nothing, and did not judge harshly the aunt or the lines of people or their view of the Sleeping Virgin.

At the time Homero passed through this town, four years had passed in which the doctors had no idea of what might be done to restore the girl to consciousness. She didn't die, she didn't live, and the odors we referred to previously were the normal ones of body function; while the crowds were absent the girl received nutriment through a tube placed into her side, which was concealed by the white satin coverlet.

Homero had not studied medicine. Although not dissimilar disciplines, myth, literature and fairy-tale gave him no authority to judge medical events presented in the interior patio, or the years that passed for the girl, now eighteen years old, a virgin indeed. As he left the Home of the Sleeping Virgin and wandered through the small town he considered deeply the implications of such a sleep, a coma as we understand it, and the passage of time without passion, without thought, and most unbearably, perhaps without dreams. How did the girl fare, beneath her crown of white flowers which were refreshed daily, and her satin coverlet of white which hid her feeding tube, and her well-manicured pale fingers with their rosary folded upon her chest? This lack of dreams was not mentioned in the Sleeping Beauty fairy-tale.

Homero continued on his journey, which truthfully was not to explore the strange and wonderful culture of his native land, but to find the birth village of his father who had recently died and left to Homero a parcel of land, which Homero must claim or forfeit. So he traveled in a leisurely way by many buses, to arrive at that coastal village his father had abandoned as a very young man. It was a journey of neither myth nor medicine, but simply a trip to claim a parcel of land, a trip on which he often dozed and dreamed odd dreams, before alighting from the bus to view another town similar with flowers, adorned shrines and patient people bringing secret prayers and arthritis.

Once the parcel was claimed, what would he do with it? Ah, but that was quite another challenge. Homero had no desire, at least not at this moment, to occupy a parcel near the hot and frothy sea, the sea which to be sure held its own myths and enchantments, but in a place so humid, so rank with decay, so overwhelmingly hot that as a very young man the father of Homero fled northward. In later years the father told the son no more than this: The sun is so hot we lived within sleep.

Homero arrived at the tiny village of his father in the early morning, crossing by hired boat a small lagoon where crocodiles and parrots occupied the water and the air, and vine-encumbered trees all the remainder between. Where the boat landed, a large hut perched, made of woven bamboo secured with vines. Nearby, several women and men sat or slowly strolled. The air was so still it seemed the very breath of the Sleeping Virgin which disturbed nothing, not even the mosquito netting suspended above her form.

Homero made inquiries, and after some hours a man was located who knew the whereabouts of the records, but perhaps they might be useless because many years ago during a tempest all the records had been drowned in their wooden chest, floating about on the lagoon until nudged ashore by crocodiles, or perhaps pulled by the twine which secured the chest, by helpful birds. In any case, the records were placed on stones and dried, but all the ink had vanished, and the papers retained only the same odor of decay as the rest of the coast, and the red wax seals of certain officials now dead.

Homero then made inquiry if anyone knew of Homero Sanchez Gomez who had left the town when still very young, leaving behind his parcel of land. The women suggested Homero the son return to the nearby town to sleep while a search was conducted, as certainly they must consult many people older than themselves. Homero understood it was time for sleep, to be in a cooler spot sheltered from the midday heat. But he hesitated to employ the small boatman to slip back through the warm water and crocodiles between the vine-encumbered trees. Perhaps he might rest here, in the protection of the bamboo hut? This was agreed, and Homero accepted the use of a hammock suspended in a shady area. Nevertheless it was terribly hot, and the odor of decay sat heavily inside his nostrils, and his shirt clung to his chest as he lay on the hammock with his hands folded, dreaming the most desultory of dreams.

When Homero woke it was close to four o'clock, and the same women were searing fish on a metal grill over a wood fire. Homero wondered how they could tolerate being near the fire, but he heard no more than the usual soft singing and women's chatter. When he rose from the hammock a woman brought him a plate, and a punctured coconut with a straw inserted through the hole.

And my father's parcel? He inquired. Yes, he was told, such a parcel in such a name did exist, but since the records were washed clean nobody now remembers where the parcel lay. It could be almost any spot, because long stretches of both the coast and the lagoon lie open and unoccupied. Perhaps he could simply choose a place he liked, and the town would certainly agree. But would he live here? What would he do with this chosen parcel? They inquired in the most polite of voices.

Ah, Homero thought, first I must choose. So he looked on both sides of the lagoon, walking a long distance through the wet sand, and finally returning to the hut without a selection. He must sleep.

The next morning he set out again, and now he found a small ridge, a small distance inland from the west, and decided this was his parcel. On it he must place a marker to signify ownership. This he intended to be a bier like that of the Sleeping Virgin, surrounded by flowers easily enough since they grew in natural profusion, and sheltered from rain by a canopy like the one that sheltered the Sleeping Virgin during the rainy season. All of this Homero accomplished in only six days time, sleeping in the hut on the hammock and eating fish and tortillas and drinking coconut milk. Each morning he stepped down to the ocean side of the beach to bathe, shedding his clothing and turning his body under the waves so that in his ears he heard the deep song of the female sea.

But then, who or what was to sleep upon the bed, which in this case was covered not with white satin, that being saved for First Communion and wedding gowns, but with a simple fish net Homero found upon the beach. The fish net was white with salt and bleached from the sun; it was soft and pliant, and to Homero's fingers it clung like a fragile soon-to-be-forgotten dream. The mosquito net hung like a gentle cloud.

Who or what was to be the Sleeping Virgin waiting for the archangel, or if you prefer, Sleeping Beauty waiting to be wakened by the kiss of a wealthy prince? Homero explained his vision to the women at the hut, but not surprisingly none volunteered for the role. Nor was there anyone in the village old enough, or comatose, soon to die.

But at last it was clear to the village folk that Homero himself would not stay and occupy his parcel, that it would be his only by the symbol of the raised bed. And the eternal sleeper, the eternal dreamer, who slept forever without death, Sleeping Virgin or Princess, what did that mean? Was this perhaps like their own story of the Mother of the Sea, who dwelled forever beneath the waves and called to bathers by day and to dreamers by night? All the villagers understood the necessity of dreams.

Now Homero set about explaining to the villagers the idea of dreams so vast and so eternal they girded the world, always repeating their story but never repeating the details. They were dreams of life emerging from deep waters and fruit hanging high in trees; dreams of ships pulled by birds to green lands; dreams of wine and loaves and fishes; dreams of winds which carry rain to young fields. And all these dreams were the same dream, and all the sleepers were the same sleeper.

The women's mouths twisted and some smiled openly. Most of their dreams were specific, concerned with staying cool, finding fish, contriving clothing with vine threads and feather adornments. They didn't understand that these were exactly the dreams to which Homero referred, because he spoke in very lofty terms due to his university education, and they understood only every other word. Nevertheless the women nodded agreement, by nature extremely polite.

Several days passed given over to discussion of the anointed dreamer, and who it might be, and why. Finally one of the women suggested a solution: that each time a baby was born the baby would sleep in daylight hours under the mosquito netting beneath the shade of the canopy, and dream whatever babies dream, so that at least part of the time the shrine would be occupied. Perhaps at times the mother might lie down with her baby on the bed, to rest a while out of the sun, and perhaps dream whatever mothers dream. Then another woman offered, perhaps when there are no babies available lovers might occupy the bed. Quickly another offered, perhaps when there are no babies and no lovers, a virgin might occupy the bed to wait and dream, and then another suggested perhaps when it came time for one of the elders to die, if there were no babies and no mothers, no lovers and no virgins, perhaps an old one could lie there to dream the soul's long journey.

All of this made a very satisfactory solution, and the village was pleased. Together they all went – and there were fifty seven people in all—to look at the well-built bier beneath its mosquito netting, with its comfortable mattress of woven fronds and its shaded canopy and its fine fishnet coverlet. It was a lovely place, what with the flowers and birds and tall vine-covered trees, near the trilling sounds of the Mother of the Sea, and the ears of those in the large hut who might hear a baby cry. Everyone nodded. They were all content, both with the resolution of Homero's parcel of land, and with his strange notions.

Homero left his parcel with its bed, and returned in the hired boat across the small lagoon where crocodiles and parrots occupied the water and the air, and vine-encumbered trees all the remainder between, to the town where he could resume his journey. Since the bus left the morning of the following day, he slept one more night in the old hotel with thick cool walls. There he dreamed a dream as full of holes as a fishnet, so that when he woke it vanished. But because of his fine education Homero understood his dream had sped to the Sleeping Virgin to comfort her, a gift freshly fashioned by Homero like a crown of white flowers to rest on her forehead. She would accept his dream because all dreams are suitable and the same, and while she slept more dreams would surely follow, finding her from the parcel of land inherited from his father.

Less than a year later Homero prepared to marry. His novia was a sweet young woman whose time at the very same University was in another era than Homero's, although scarcely eight years later. Homero's widowed mother rejoiced that her son was marrying, and of course she dreamed of grandchildren, not caring much if they would be boys or girls, but only that they might be healthy, and noted as hers.

Homero went to the priest of his novia with two good friends to swear and testify that Homero was not already married, nor a father, nor a drunkard. He went to the pre-nuptial benediction the parents of his novia hosted, and listened patiently to the readings of two dozen injunctions, and accepted two dozen gifts, and two dozen blessings placed on his head and shoulders by the aunts and uncles and cousins while he and his novia knelt side by side on a red velvet cushion. As for the wedding itself, the widowed mother of Homero arranged it with similar regard for tradition, and the celebratory dinner following also portrayed exemplary decorum and respect for the long customs of his native culture.

Imagine the surprise then, when his young bride voiced a request that they travel after their wedding night somewhere really fun and have a blast; their honeymoon was what she referred to.

Well and good. The bride, whose name was Elisabeta, sugested Huatulco, a resort town of tourists and salsa, beaches and bars. Certainly a blast, and furthermore, Elisabeta assured him, they would have access to internet cafés and would be in touch with their mothers and friends. Homero could think of no reason why not, and agreed.

After the wedding night—and without embarrassment I assure you neither was virginal, due to changes in the times - they set off by bus on the slow trip south. Now came many hours in which to chat, eat fruit, and doze hand in hand on the soft first-class seats. Elisabeta confided to Homero that she would like to finish her graduate studies before having children. She was taking the pill and studying marine biology. Homero inquired if she was familiar with the story of the Mother of the Sea, and related his experience of locating his father's parcel of land. To his surprise—it seemed married life held no end of surprises—Elisabeta suggested they pause in their journey to visit the Sleeping Virgin, and this would be a fine moment for Homero to check on the efficacy of the dreams he hoped were finding their way to the Virgin as she lay with flowers circling her forehead. As for the Mother of the Sea, of course everyone who studied marine biology received and understood this information. Elisabeta said the Mother was referred to in text books as the birther of all life, and as Elisabeta explained evolution to Homero, he realized she had a fine education in her own department, although he understood only half of what she said.

At the Home of the Sleeping Virgin they stood in line for an hour in the well-kept living room among the reverent and docile. Elisabeta gazed at the several Saints and pictures of Mary and Jesus and made sure her two pesos were ready in her pocket. Homero, for his part, awaited his glimpse of the Virgin. Now here was yet another challenge—how could one know if a person comatose for five years had during the past year begun to dream? It was not possible that she had dreamed before his intervention. But now, did she dream? And how would he know? As they stood in line, he looked at his young bride as a husband might, and wondered what dreams did his bride dream? And she responded, I? I dream of finding below the waves the First Child of the Mother of the Sea. And how could that be? Elisabeta replied, perhaps not the Child itself, but news of the Child. And she smiled sweetly at her husband.

Alas, their view of the Sleeping Virgin was not satisfactory. The mosquito netting had become heavier perhaps, or perhaps the sun was in a different quarter. The form was shadowed, remote; and those who genuflected and crossed their torsos and kissed their thumbs did so only on faith. Beneath the white shield of satin and netting it was no longer possible to see the Virgin's crown nor her form, and certainly not her expression, nor her possible smile. As they left Elisabeta said wisely, She must be close to death. And that was quite true. The aunt could no longer expect visitors to sigh in awe at the sight of her niece's serene face and silent manicured fingers. The doctors reported only that as they had not known why the Sleeping Virgin lived, they did not know now why she lay on the same bier dying, but for almost a year now surely her serene form had declined, and her serene face gathered lines.

As they left the Home of the Sleeping Virgin and wandered through the small town Homero considered deeply the implications of the change. Perhaps her days no longer passed without passion and without thought. If the Sleeping Virgin now dreamed, time must be evident in the dreams sent to her, dreams from babies and mothers, and lovers and virgins, and those ancient ones preparing for the soul's journey. How did the girl fare with this movement ferried by dreams from the sea, and captured beneath her crown of white flowers? Homero could not know.

Thereafter, despite Elisabeta's willingness to go the town of Homero's father to see his parcel of land, Homero did not choose to take his bride to the lagoon. Instead they rode on, down the coast on the fashionable side to where the hotels of Huatulco have swimming pools to protect bathers from the rank odors of the coast, and the air-conditioned rooms make it possible to remain awake at midday, and play cards or view from the balcony the turquoise waters and cruise ships approaching in the distance. At night they went to a bar and tapped their feet while listening to music, and they enjoyed sipping through straws plunged into coconuts, and dining on freshly caught fish. When they went to bed, on a fine broad mattress adorned with a white satin bridal suite cover, they made love and dreamed a dream which traveled back and forth between them, always the same but with different details.

When they woke the next day Elisabeta informed her new husband they must walk away from the hotel to find the sea. Homero wore his swimming trunks beneath his clothing so when they came to the shore he could insert his body into the waves and hear the voice he remembered, the Mother of the Sea. Elisabeta wore her bikini, and brought her snorkel gear so that she could peer below the waves. She hoped she might see an eel or a coelacanth.

This all occurred as planned, and they wandered alone, the only two people occupying the beach as the morning sun twisted itself into vines on the tall trees. Elisabeta beneath the waves saw schools of yellow and blue cunning little fish, and the toes of her husband which kept falling into her view. Homero heard the song of the sea, and the frail bubbles of his bride's breath breaking on the surface when they rose.

When they returned satisfied to the hotel at midday the television was announcing that the Sleeping Virgin had died that morning in the little town where her aunt reduced the price to one peso to see the bier where the Sleeping Virgin had formerly slept. The television camera showed the mosquito net canopy, and the white satin coverlet, and the patio beautiful with flowers and birds. Homero wished they would show the face of the Virgin, but instead they showed a serious doctor who stated nothing of this was a miracle, the girl had simply expired.

Nevertheless thousands from the town walked with her funeral cortege the next day, while the band played and children carried bunches of white flowers, as Homero could see on the bright television screen, because like dreams, certain events always repeat their story although never with the same details.

recycling benjie

Just the title of this story should tell you that Benjie is dead. Benjie never anchored. When he and Gemini met, it was she who floated, if one can float upstairs to a balcony, but it was Benjie who floated down. In their flows, coming and going, it was clear that neither of them attached to the activities of the university. They sat literally above it all, not precisely disdainful, but not belonging.

"What are you doing up here?" Gemini asked when she reached the landing of the balcony and spotted the lean Benjie slouched in a velvet theater chair. She already was failing in her task of monitoring the actors' voices from a distance, tuning her ear to this other voice.

"Nothing" he replied, and it was true. Outwardly Benjie was doing nothing, although later Gemini came to realize he did everything on the inside, a brain protected by bone and a dark thatch. Like most young men he wore a Tee shirt and jeans, and that was his natural costume. Youth, non-compliant, unattached. Much later Gemini also realized he would never relinquish a Tee shirt he loved, and he loved them all, long after armpit hairs began to sprout through gaping seams, and no acquaintance remembered the significance of the slogans.

"Save Adelphi Square? Hey, man, who was Adelphi Square? Played bass, right? In the eighties, right? Went to prison for five years on possession, right?" Wrong on all counts. Benjamin himself couldn't recall, but vaguely he knew in his ripped and damaged Tee-shirt-covered-bosom that Adelphi Square was significant, truly symbolic, one might say, of the ills to which Benjie and his cohort of neo-liberalism's children refused to succumb.

Benjamin died wearing a Tee shirt. Gemini could not recall having seen him in any other attire since about two hours after the marriage ceremony which sucked them like under-the-sofa dust, out of the crowd of other young people and into their singular coupled existence. In the country club's cream-and gold bathroom Benjie whipped off his cummerbund, ruffled shirt, black tie, jacket and pants, opened a brown grocery bag and donned jeans and Tee shirt. Hand in hand with his bride he danced his way out of the life of wealth his parents and hers had so yearningly fantasized. Gemini recalled the sadness on her father's face as Benjie happily performed some kind of unidentifiable movements in his declaration of freedom clothing. The band failed to play any waltz or foxtrot. They were gone.

Gemini didn't exactly regret the Tee-shirt attitude of her spouse, but they never had quite enough money, not even when he wrote programs for Microsoft, or when she accepted the post of director of fundraising for Acne Power. Well, that wasn't the real name of the youth group she worked for, long past the age when she herself could be called a youth. It was located at a YMCA hung out to dry in a shabby area of Seattle, and everyone who worked there, the young and the not-so-young, wore a Tee shirt, with colors and graphics and slogans and sizes which melded in her mind with those worn by Benjie, so that some nights as he pulled off his daily attire she wasn't sure until he lay next to her in bed that he was her individual without a Tee shirt, familiar to her hands during thirty years of happiness.

They were that unreasonable kind of couple who got along, and once the idea of having babies was put aside, they lived a remarkably carefree and mobile life as non-consumers. With no kids, they didn't require a house or car; they didn't need to save for college educations or dread empty-nest syndrome. They were free to try life on a communal farm (two years, got tired of green beans), free to investigate Bali (one year, ran out of funds) free to spin away on their tandem bike to see the Atlantic up close, and bike back to Seattle when they'd seen it. Then they were free to abandon the USA altogether when imperialism became unbearable, and they fled south the Mexico.

By then they both could work exclusively by internet, Gemini concocting fund-raising appeals and grant applications for not-for-profits who could pay, and Benjamin doing the same for software. And nobody even knew where they were!

On their fiftieth birthdays, celebrated on a single day to simplify matters, Gemini bought Benjie a Tee shirt which carried a stylized print of Ricardo Flores Magón on the front, an anarchist A symbol on the back. Not that they were anarchists; they were anarchists by default, that is, they hadn't yet brought themselves to espouse any form or method of governance handed out at any time or place they were familiar with. The closest they approached to a system, those two unsystematized persons, was the comunalidad they encountered in the state of Oaxaca, an indigenous rejection of ethnocide based on common ownership of land coupled to one of the sixteen indigenous languages that still survived. These were secret languages, each like kids speaking uppy-duppy, like with your de-coder ring. With deep respect for the privacy of others, they never tried to learn. They learned the colonizers' language, Spanish, and settled in the sunshine in their customary manner, birds on a wire, unidentifiable migrants.

That same birthday anniversary, Benjie gave Gemini a jar of organic mango jelly. As usual Benjie always was prepared to move on down the highway; he assumed they would travel light, not owning anything that couldn't be consumed within an hour or left behind. Thus he always gifted Gemini with food or soap, their two basic consumables. Gemini owned two pairs of sandals and one pair of sneakers, her half of their tandem bike, two blouses and two jeans, one for dress-up and one for daily. Sometimes she yearned for more, but never admitted to Benjie her desires. It would have been somehow disloyal. She knew that Benjie carried inside his thatch-covered brain all his world. He didn't and wouldn't possess more, so why should she?

But only three years later Benjie lay dead, in fact, dead only some hours. The formalities of his chauffeured route to the crematorium were arranged. Gemini sent one e-mail to everyone on her list, which included Ben's eighty-year old father and her own sister. No service would be held, and nobody would fly to Oaxaca to hold her hand in the moment of bereavement. She wasn't even bereaved yet, it was too soon. But something else within her was at work: her anger at Benjie for being dead, an invisible substance in the atmosphere where he previously sat visible. This anger coupled to anger at having no nice clothes, by which she meant pretty widow clothes like other women seemed to wear and discard after each TV funeral. She never wanted those things, did she? But she didn't want Benjie to assume (retrospectively) that she didn't want them, to have them available for the not-happening death and the not-happening funeral and the not-happening public display of grief of a woman connected to a family and community, comforted.

She didn't want to own a collection of Tee shirts either. But now she inherited all of Benjie's wealth: a laptop, half a tandem bicycle, and forty-seven Tees. And there wouldn't even be a funeral, just legal paperwork for the USA government, a useless act of submission to bureaucracy. No will existed because Benjie left as a trace of himself nothing more than a half-used bar of Venus Rosa bath soap; self-employed, he never filed income tax or paid social security. That was their agreement, and Gemini had her own social security from the days she functioned as a paid employee. But she never filed, not then nor now.

Benjie had sloughed off his non-participatory life, including forty-seven clean Tee shirts. Gemini lifted them out of the box they inhabited, and place them on the table in front of her. What now? She gathered them in her arms and lay down with the soft fabric on the bed they had shared. The smell was of laundry, not of Benjie. He was well and truly vanished. Gemini regained her feet and went to look in the bathroom: Benjie's toothbrush, his black comb. She took them with her back to the bed and slept with Benjie's legacy tucked into her stomach like an unborn child.

When the phone woke her she dutifully responded to the crematorium's pleasant request for instructions. Yes she would take the ashes, In a cardboard box, please. Thank you. I will come to collect the box. Yes, this morning.

Gemini showered and pulled on her dress-up jeans. And then, since nobody cared, she donned the top Tee shirt from the pile still body-warm on the bed, a red shirt with STOP THE WAR stenciled on the front. Which war? It didn't matter. For Benjie, that war was over. She took the next one, a faded yellow that said LIFE IS SWEET and simply pulled it on top of WAR. However, under the circumstances it didn't seem appropriate. She couldn't recall if Benjie owned a Tee that said LIFE WAS SWEET BUT NOW I'M DEAD. Probably not. One by one she took the shirts and drew them over her head and down her torso, gradually losing her own form, submerged in multi-colors. After fifteen she wondered briefly if she would be able to move her arms, covered in fifteen different sleeves of fifteen different faded colors. By the time she had donned thirty Tees her waist had vanished, and her neck felt hot. At forty-seven she stopped. Nothing further presented itself. Shapeless and stout, with a protruding bosom like a soft pillow, like a woman who had born too many children, she had donned her entire Benjie.

With the sandals on her feet and her bag over her shoulder she presented herself at the crematorium office adjoining a clean bland reception room with polished pewter floor candelabra supporting thick white candles. Not for her. Dimly she heard the voices of mourners, in a more remote sala, perhaps one man's sobbing, a deep throb of despair. She wondered if Benjie would have sobbed if the heat attack felled her instead of him. Mercifully a quick instant death, one moment fine, the next an alarmed gasping, and then a strange stare, as if to ask, Who are you? Who am I? But he now filled a blue cardboard box, bone and ash, almost gift-wrapped, neat and attractive. The box was neatly sealed, as if the crematorium man never imagined her opening it to inspect the remains, perhaps putting her fingers in to separate a fragment which then she would have made into a necklace... not. She acknowledged the box with a nod. She signed the forms. She accepted documents confirming Benjie's demise, with cause, date and place certified by the crematorium's own doctor. These she folded neatly to fit into her shoulder bag, and pulled out the correct sum of pesos in a clean white envelope, which she handed over to the undertaker with another brief nod of acknowledgement—their business completed. Then she picked up the cardboard container. It weighed maybe two kilos, less than the weight of forty-seven Tee shirts on her sweating body. She trundled herself and the package out the door, down the steps, down the sidewalk and into the nearby park, where she placed her sweating body on a bench cemented in place beneath the canopy of a centenarian tree, next to a teen-ager who looked at her with curious dark eyes. Marginally cooler. With the sealed box of ashes next to her on the bench, she peeled off the outer Tee shirt. I LOVE NY it said. The young fellow picked it up. "Very nice," he said. "Not too big." "Do you want it? Permit me to give you it as a gift", responded Gemini. She was already pulling over her head the next shirt, and by the time she got it off, pushed her hair from her face, and freed her vision, the kid was gone. Not gone. Seated on the stone fountain rim he displayed his new Tee shirt to some buddies, and pointed in her direction.

Another kid came. He stopped in front of her and asked, "Are you giving away this Tee shirt?" It was a rather non-descript dark green, with a design on it and print no longer legible. "Yes, of course". As the boy smiled and moved toward the group at the fountain Gemini took off the next shirt. She wondered if there were forty-seven kids there, or if she would have to wait until they sent for the rest of their acquaintances, or no, maybe girls would like a shirt. How long does it take to remove forty-seven Tee shirts? And hand them over, receiving a smile and a thank you? Hours later Gemini was down to her own blouse, stained with sweat under the armpits. She could feel the damp spot on her back immediately start to dry in the heavy afternoon sun. After a long while she sighed. She stood up and wondered exactly where she should go with her new-found lightness, her still shapeless but slenderized body. By habit she turned to Benjie to ask his opinion, but Benjie was gone. Which of the parade of youngsters had scooped him up in his cardboard container, and where had he been carried off to? A little wobbly on her feet, she was. Abruptly she sat again on the same bench. She looked under the bench and behind the bench. The box had vanished. Who would open it, thinking maybe it contained some other American treasure, and what would become of

Benjie's remains? How amazing. One day she had a spouse, and her spouse in turn owned forty-seven Tee shirts, and at least two kilos of mineral weight minus fluids. All gone. For five thousand pesos, Gemini had reached total bereavement.

She gazed around. The square seemed filled with adolescents wearing richly colored and sloganized Tee shirts. And perhaps dust, floating like pollen. Or maybe she imagined the dust. Ruffling her hair she rested her head against the bench back and closed her eyes. A light breeze brushed her bare arms. Then with no warning the bells of the city's forty-seven churches thronged across the sky like birds flocking homeward to roost. Gemini wondered if the bells called worshipers to six o'clock mass, or warned of an earthquake she could not yet feel. She didn't open her eyes. Quietly she waited to learn what comes next.

Vignettes

tbe roco~rolo tree

Pilgrim's Progress, Oaxaca Chirtmas, 1999

The "modern" clock-face installed on the south wall of the Cathedral refuses to proceed past 2:00; but the government powers-that-be are very timely. Beneath the clock on the south side of the Cathedral plaza, they erected a Coca-Cola Tree. A white iron rail barrier protects it, along with a replica of a cozy wooden cottage where one presumes Santa and his dear wife and elves might live.

December 22: the handsome old colonial zocalo and plaza are thronged. Overhead the brilliant full moon, final full moon of year, of the century, of the millenium, depending on whose calendar you choose. Lots of amateurs, cooks and craftspeople, women who sew blouses, string amber beads, weave hats - the whole population has turned out, to sell or buy. Housewives brought their own comals, ceramic cooking discs that balance on top of charcoal stoves. Tortilla presses, transported away from homes, do service in the plaza. The odor of grilled meats saturates the air. The sugared fruits and cream-filled pastries swarm with bees.

Coca-Cola Christmas Trees grow in Mexico. We saw the first of the season in Campeche: a high plastic green thing onto which were pegged huge round red disks, each proclaiming "Coca-Cola". The current PAN candidate for president used to work for Coke, but I'm sure his personal attention was not required, so prevalent is the government scramble to "modernize" the economy. The domination of corporate icons, from Coke to Disney, is putting Tommy Hilfiger on the back of the eager Mexican consumer, and Nikes on his feet; alert PRI officials stand with open arms.

But perhaps something this year went too far.

One of the oldest cathedrals of Mexico graces the Oaxaca plaza. The first was built in Mexico DF, the second in Puebla, the third in Oaxaca. The first two have been damaged by settling and earthquakes. The Oaxaca cathedral, its weather-scrubbed statuary on the high frieze, the mosaic of dark and light tiles on its twin domed belfries, the grand walls, is virtually intact. It has a name, but no-one seems to know it; simply it's called La Catedrál, the Cathedral.

Flash over to the main zocalo, where romp a couple of plaster polar bears (sort of like dinosaurs for crazed Oaxacan children), twin plaster snowmen, and beyond them, a Nativity scene. It appears quite traditional until you see that in front of it, two outsized Disney-type Easter bunnies pour water from jugs into an artificial pool.

The evening before Noche de Los Rabanos, Night of The Radishes, George and I strolled down to see the plaza fill with stalls of hand-made crafts, foods, sweets, music, the munificent and animated display which makes Oaxaca so enjoyable. Not a square foot of the plaza or surrounding streets lay empty. Meanwhile the city government had started installation of special plywood display areas for the radishes, and on most of them children were bounced around trampoline style, dashing back and forth. We ascended to a restaurant above the square for dinner and a glass of Noche Buena, the Christmas-only beer. Gazing down from the open balcony window past the strings of Christmas lights, I realized the Coca-Cola Tree was gone.

The Spanish word is lovely: se quitó; they were quit of it.

Just that morning we read in Reforma, a major Mexican daily, a diatribe pointing out the gross violation of any cultural sense of self in Oaxaca's holiday decorations. The article was one of several complaints about despoiling Oaxaca's heritage.

Okay. So we say to the waiter, "What happened to the Coca-Cola Tree?" and he replied, in a fairly forthcoming way, that many people didn't like it, and furthermore, that with it in place, there was no space for the radishes. "Ah," we responded, knowing full-well that radish ramps had surrounded the polar bears and bunnies in the square, "Did you see the news article in today's Reforma?" No, he hadn't. Off he went to borrow a copy from the owner, who did have one.

Meanwhile at the table next to us, appeared three men in business attire, two of them chained to cell phones. Our area of the restaurant was now emptying of customers. Calls were made. The waiter reappeared and said the owner's copy of Reforma was not to be found. A bustle behind George with waiters and tables. Then entered four more gents in suits, one of whom I recognized as the Municipal President, and another surely the Governor. They began their discussion.

So perhaps we were inadvertent witnesses to a meeting of the cabal, during which I hope recriminations were issued in regard to the Coca-Cola Tree fiasco. But more likely, plots were laid to further implicate Oaxaca in cultural self-destruction. Speaking only as a tourist, and leaving aside the miseries imposed by neoliberalism, I don't think these official guys are too bright. One of the grand facts of the festival, I felt, is that although consumerism runs rampant, much is hecho por mano, hand made, so when I spend money I'm giving it directly to the worker, not to a remote owner/profit-taker. Except of course for Coke.

Downstairs as we left, a man braced himself against the doorway walls as if for a long night. When we passed, I asserted, without really knowing, "That guy's a security cop." Intrepid George returned to the man and asked him if he was guarding the Municipal President. "No," he replied, "the Governor." Just to make sure, we returned in twenty minutes and there he still stood. A long night.

So what's the radish story?

The Night of the Radishes is an authentic folk custom, proceeding from a competition among flower-growers and horticulturists. Apparently the first event a hundred years ago took place at a Christmas Vigil market, and it just grew, as good folk customs do. The main ingredient is radishes, extravagantly carved to represent animals and figures. I mean, not just one radish, but a sculpture of radishes, with some radishes opened flat to create stars, some carved with faces and costumes, and some skinned to make replicas of wood shingles or planks. Carts and stars! Pageants, parades, murals depicting the Nativity, historical events, saints, horses, dancers and dreams: radishes on top of radishes, a veritable Radish Renaissance! Dried corn husks are dyed and twisted to make costumes for the figures; entire montages are constructed with vegetables and flowers. Judges and spectators proceed around the ramps. Comments are exchanged; photos taken; kind translations offered; even the security guard responded to my question: "It's a scene of harvesting the maize," - depicted in corn skin, of course. Our favorite in the corn skin category was a plaza scene, complete with umbrella-shaded tables, strolling vendors and families, the Cathedral, of course. In the radish category, what we liked best was a frog riding on the back of a turtle. The caption was, "Different Destinations." Prizes, music - the whole event is astonishing and enjoyable. And then capped off with fireworks.

By then the fire brigade had arrived, with their yellow helmets and windbreaker jackets zipped to the neck. Each man was armed with a small red fire extinguisher, and circulated on foot through the stalls and streets, alert and ready. I noticed as we made our way around toward the Cathedral, a platform set up for viewing the fireworks, with firework armatures neatly arranged. They stood in the Coca-Cola Tree's vacated space.

The tradition of El Noche de Los Rabanos precedes the tourist industry as surely as Christmas does, but of course tourists streamed everyplace. Tourists buy the embroidered blouses, draw-string pants, ribbon-bedecked dresses. Young Oaxaqueños wear Levis, older folks basic polyester, the wealthier in today's Mexico City mode. The locals eat street food, often a terror to tourists who head for the tourist restaurants where foods are disinfected.

So now, still filled with Coca-Cola righteous indignation, I need a Reality Check. What Reality Check are you referring to here, Dearie? asks my alter ego. Questions for which I have no answers, THAT reality. For example, at what point in our history did a North Pole with elves appear in a Filene's Department Store window, and become instantly acceptable in Boston? Or kosher Chinese restaurants?

On Christmas Eve we straggled out of our apartment clad in Chiapas-made woolies, and in addition I pulled my hecho por mano rebozo around the shoulders of my hecho por mano jacket. It was cold—maybe 52° Fahrenheit. Overhead the moon still gleamed, somewhat worn around the edges. We walked the dark street until we heard music, and like children to the Pied Piper, followed until we were caught up in a procession.

To explain Mexican processions, their main aspect is that they too are hecho por mano, with an assembled band of musicians followed by an assembled troop of ordinary folks. For Christmas, this procession included a young girl mounted on a burro, her white satin mantle draped over her head and around the burro's flanks. Three men on horses followed, costumed with charming fake whiskers and crowns, to represent the Wise Men. Behind came the people, carrying torches made of candles mounted inside cellophane shades on long sticks, and sparklers throwing points of light recklessly upon us. I accepted a torch from an unknown woman; we were smiled at, spoken to, a part of the procession.

We paraded down to the zocalo, our small troop meeting up with grander ones that qualify as calendas because they included floats: trucks bearing an assortment of angels secured with ropes to little chairs on the back of the truck, bigger angels seated in front of Nativity scenes, biggest angels of all standing serious with the Annunciation. The bands bur-burped, crowds lined the streets admiring the halos and wings; shoulder to shoulder we swept along. Finally, halted in the crowd, a little boy asked for our torch, and it was handed over. George blew out the fire that immediately ensued, and so we were released from the magic spell.

Reality Check, please.

The spectators milled about, eating whatever, watching dancing figures of huge frame and papier-mâché puppets, held aloft by twirling young men. Their puppets of mustachioed men and pink-cheeked women bobbed and turned, approached the circled crowd, retreated; someone ignited firework wheels; I protected my hair with my rebozo.

Instead of waiting for Midnight Mass in The Cathedral, George and I headed back toward our apartment by way of Santo Domingo, where an earlier mass was already in progress. I listened for a while to the song and response in Spanish. Then we all exchanged the Christmas Kiss of Peace, the traditional embrace, handshakes. When the congregation began to move forward to take Communion, I left. I arrived home to find George ahead of me, eating a sandwich.

On Christmas day I returned to the zocalo. On my way down I spotted Elisabeta on her bicycle heading toward the hardware shop; a mother riding side-saddle behind her daughter on a motor bike. The markets are open.

The zocalo stalls began business; a few food vendors already stirred meat and chilled the bottles of Coca-Cola. In the area of the Cathedral's south side fireworks and platforms were gone; one of those mysterious feats of setting up and taking down so common here. Instead, in the swept open area, a few raggedy-ass little boys played at baseball.

I found my friend Virginia in her clothing stall, sitting on the floor with her two children, eating a cactus fruit. She was wearing her saleswoman clothes: an indigenous wool wrap long skirt and a madly-striped red over-blouse. Her little girl also wore the over-blouse; beneath it showed the ruffles of her dress. Virginia and I had made an agreement to exchange English/Spanish lessons. Today she explained to me that she buys her stock of blouses and pants from a woman in her village. She pays as little as possible, and sells them in the market for as much as she can. "For example", she said, "I bought those pants for fifteen, and I'll sell them for thirty." So I began with the numbers, twenty, thirty, forty, fifty...

Sadly our lesson came to an end when her little girl fell into a fountain. She was pulled out wailing, damp and chilled. Virginia bustled the child into the stall, comforted her, changed her into a little jersey pants set topped with a matching blouse with Mickey on the front, and then a sweater. We arranged to meet again next week.

I went to eat. Fearless. I sat at a stall and ate first a Styrofoam cupful of corn soup with lime juice, cheese and chili powder. Great. I followed up with an empanada stuffed with cheese and squash flowers; watched the cook behind her comal, flanked by her husband. Seated on the bench next to me was a young Mexican woman from Veracruz. I asked them how they had liked the Coca-Cola Tree and polar bears. The cook had no opinion; she's a professional and so busy cooking she never went half a block down the street to see the zocalo display. The Veracruz woman thinks Coca-Cola advertises too much, to which the husband and wife agree. But she harbored no bad feelings about polar bears and snowmen, which don't replace the Nativity scene. I drank a bowl of heavily-sugared coffee Mexican style, and chewed my empanada. The conversation wound down. "There have never been polar bears here," they told me, "nor snow". "Never?" I inquired. "No, never," they insisted, "not in the history of Oaxaca, nor in the history of Mexico."

"But do you have snow in the United States?" I admitted that we do. "And do you miss it?" I admitted that I do not. "The climate in Oaxaca is very nice, no?" Yes, I agreed, it's very nice.

We parted with pleasant wishes for a Happy Christmas. By the time I reached our street, the day's thumping bands and truckloads of angels already were in motion, although I couldn't tell where they were going. The sound of music followed into our apartment, seemingly coming from every direction.

tlacolula

17 October, 1999

Those of you who enjoy the decor of my apartment on Beacon Hill will be happy to know the challenge of our little Oaxaca place is gradually achieving solution. For one thing, by a stroke of enormous good fortune the walls in both the living-room and kitchen are exactly the color of masking tape, permitting us to obscure some of the gouges made in the plaster by the prior removal of dozens of nails. We ignore those still evident everywhere. I'm happy to report I reduced the number of sombreros on the walls from eight to three, and the crates tacked to the walls to just one. This latter I achieved by taking down the other five and stacking them in the space in the vertical crèche in the living room wall. As yet we have no particular books, but the radio nicely fills one "shelf".

Today George and I went to Tlacolula, a village about half an hour's bus ride from Oaxaca. We crammed into the bus with too many others, and most of the way stood admiring the scenery over the shoulder of the driver. Oaxaca sits in a valley where three plains conjoin, and around us loom the Sierras on every side. The ride to Tlacolula is level, following the international highway which is two lanes wide and a bit choppy, although the driver said the ruts were not caused by the recent earthquakes, not the biggest nor the thirty-three aftershocks. Just road in disrepair. So that was fine.

We disembarked at the Tlacolula bus station, which has a remarkably fine bathroom, for those of you who, like me, take serious note of public bathrooms. This one had toilet seats, doors on the stalls, and in mid-morning was quite clean, with a sink with water running in two of the four spigots, for washing hands. The toilet-paper person was on duty, so for just two pesos one could buy paper if necessary; of course I carry my own supplies since not all facilities are as adequate. They must keep it for the vast number of visitors.

Today was market day. The bus station empties directly into the midst of the stalls and wares, every variety of items imaginable in somewhat the style of our lost Woolworth's plus foods, filling the road on both sides so that we could barely pass. Foreign tourists were few; the Oaxacans were out in force to buy at auction pots and blankets, to eat the sweets and lunch foods, to examine hats and shoes, to finger plastic tablecloths and buckets, to admire dishes and ceramics. We toured the market, bought lunch at a stall and ate it sitting on a wall. George's was a sandwich; we recognized that. Our sense of adventure with food is holding well; since that first week's trip to the hospital nothing unexpected has occurred.

Afterward we went for a walk, the town is smaller by its sense of intimacy and indigenous population, more than by it physical size. We did observe some local people taking taxis. These taxis are bicycles pulling a high square carriage topped with a canvas roof for shade. The passengers sit quite upright, and seem to be enjoying a lark as we do in a horse-drawn carriage; in fact, the scene looked similar in all respects except the lack of horse-droppings. On the rear of each vehicle is a sign promoting its ecological benefits.

The cathedral, like most we see, has round Moorish-style domes, implanted with ceramic tiles. The interior ceilings are baroque, and intricately gilded, but outside the stone seems as weathered as if it were the original from 1590, despite years of earthquakes. We sat in one of the four naves for half an hour's rest out of the sun, watching the parade of Oaxacans drift in and out. Many carried long-stemmed flowers such as gladiola and carnations, which they brushed against the legs and reachable parts of the crucified Jesus and various other saints. These flowers were carried home as we saw on the return bus journey; touching a saint is dusting for blessings, and when the flowers release their scent in the home, their blessings scatter in the air. For the most part the church afforded, as do all the churches we have entered, a peaceful respite for informal family groups. People genuflected and then rested, some prayed in a nonchalant way; a man read in the pew behind us. When we left we refreshed ourselves further by buying the local popsicles, and Coca-Cola emptied into a plastic bag with a straw emerging from the knotted neck (this is to avoid having to pay for or return the bottle.)

From the church we rejoined the crowd in the zocalo, where a concert was in progress. I must admit I'm a fool for mariachi. Those falling notes, that whine for love, those falsetto cries of pain! I love it. We enjoyed more than an hour, sitting in chairs arranged for the public in the concert space, while three musicians stood at their microphones looking hot and uncomfortable in suit jackets and neckties. They sang along with their guitars and bass, but even better were the guest singers, two men who obviously enjoyed a strong local following. Each song was sincerely applauded, sometimes during an exceptionally well-sustained falsetto note, and each was followed by cries of otra, otra, more, more. George was so enchanted that after we left the music he offered to purchase a tapestry rug, one of the thousands dyed and woven by hand by local artisans. We selected a scene of a village, with houses, women carrying baskets on their heads, and a lively pig chased by a man in a sombrero. We hung the rug on the living room wall, thereby bringing to a close the story of at least four more nails, their holes, and some three dimensional (not tapestry) straw hats. It's a pleasant scene, and very realistic, in that the weaver captured the crooked curves of the houses, each woven in several colors; and in the background, in palest blue, stands a mountain.

You know there will be an election in Mexico also in 2,000, for the Mexican congress and president. The national government with its single ruling party would like to hang onto power, of course; it's been ruling more than seventy years. The participation of workers, poor farmers, and popular and indigenous organizations one would expect to be minimal in a country where democracy has not yet taken hold. Several of these groups can't find adequate channels of participation. The inability of the system to incorporate them into the official party's structure generated protests, thus far to no avail. But I notice that the middle-class, or those we would more accurately think of as professional-poor, take little interest. They ignore struggles for power and participation and go right to the heart of maintaining some standard of living by whatever means possible. For example, the woman who cleans my apartment once a week with her teenage daughter is doing so for extra money to send her three children to the university. They are not poor, but they see where the margin lies.

The state of Oaxaca sustains flagrant inequality and social injustice. Despite having enormous natural resources, 76% of its population lives in conditions of misery. As a consequence, a high degree of conflict and political violence has existed since remote times: land conflicts, "white guards", armed groups, etc. There's a lot of conflict generated by fraudulent electoral processes, despotic control by local bosses, and manipulation by party politicians, often bloody. It's made worse by concurrent use of two Systems of Election, both with legal recognition. One runs on rules of historic custom, "Derecho Consuetudinario" or Uses and Customs. That's the system which so fascinated us three years ago, and whose "white papers" George has been translating. The other system uses rules of political parties, "Derecho Positivo". In the last election of Municipal Authorities in October of 1998, of a total of 570 Municipalities, 418 conducted their election by Uses and Customs and 152 by political parties.

You can be sure that the government doesn't want to lose the party system, but sometimes one can't be sure which system is worse. There's no doubt that earthquake and flood relief are being withheld by the PRI (the ruling party) so that just before an election the PRI will buy votes by dispensing the aid donated by foreign governments or charities. But on the other hand, some of the traditional municipalities have entrenched families who don't make way when demographics change; new families move in but have no access to participation. So it's bad all over. Meanwhile I read in today's paper that 45% of Mexican children under the age of five suffer from malnutrition.

All this is difficult to keep in mind while we are playing tourist and having fun. On the return bus ride from Tlacolula, also overcrowded, two elderly men had fitted themselves in seats. The one who sat next to the window was lugging several packages tied up in bags with string. The old gent who sat by the aisle declined to pay his fare, for the perfect reason that he had no money. The "conductor" gave up, and the old gent settled in. He ate a tangerine he carried, spitting seeds and skin onto the bus floor. Finally he took out a yellow apple, and lacking teeth, asked us to cut it for him. I opened my Swiss Army knife and carefully dropped into George's outstretched hand seeds and core, which George in despair finally threw out the window. The old man offered each of us a section of the apple, but we declined, having taken our risks for the day. When we reached the city, the senior next to the window was ready to get off. The old gent next to the aisle refused to get up; perhaps he thought he couldn't. This man has a very deep voice with rocks rattling in it. The window man handed his packages over the heads of other passengers, and then tried to get himself over the legs of the gravel-voiced gent, who the whole while growled (in Spanish of course), "fuck you, accursed son of a whore" and more of the same which happily I understood perfectly. So did the other passengers, and everyone laughed except the man trying to get out. He succeeded finally, listing badly with his bags and poor old legs. We followed. Immediately it began to rain, and so we ran home as happy as children, toting our rug and holding up my umbrella, repeating the curses in a mimic of the baritone growl, and laughing.

Incidentally, the word for sun umbrella being parasol, it will not surprise you to learn that the word for rain umbrella is paraguas, but the rains will come to an end in a few weeks, I'm told.

where doctors make house calls

Last week I became ill. But maybe that's not the way to begin. Maybe first I should explain that I teach English privately to adults here in Oaxaca, a pleasant pastime for me, and maybe even a help to folks who for their own reasons believe they need the imperial language. Among my students is a doctor, whom I shall call Alberto, because as Alberto has told me more than once, if his wife ever catches him fooling around she'll kill him.

Alberto is not fooling around—anyway, not with me. Really, I'm entirely sure he's not. Saying his wife will kill him is a macho brag on how much his wife loves him, and from all he says they do seem to have a happy household: three kids who don't do their homework, his wife manages the money, his mother-in-law lives with them, he walks his dogs daily, etc. Alberto is a pediatric surgeon, the best in the city of Oaxaca. I have that on authority of Alberto himself.

Our classes, three hours a week, established their own ritual of coffee and intimacy. At first Alberto also included remarks regarding the beauty of my eyes and my superior intelligence, which of course I enjoyed, despite having to inform him about the culture lag. Mexico is forty or so years behind the USA, so back in Boston the student may not declare the beauty of the teacher's eyes, nor the other way around. Rather a pity. Our intimacy progressed when we discovered we share a Valentine birthday; he is twenty years my junior. On my 69th birthday he brought a lovely chocolate cake his wife shopped for, and we three with George included, ate cake for breakfast, and I presented Alberto with a home-made birthday card, first ascertaining from a local friend if it is alright to address a pediatrician as mi galán without inciting his wife to sharpen her knives. So we progressed.

One day Alberto, in the course of declaiming something or other in English, assured me that were I ever to fall ill, he would be happy to attend me. "But," says I, "you are a pediatric surgeon (which of course he knew), and I am a person of the third age" (as senescence is so gently referred to in Mexico). "Yes," he replied, "but I also take care of my mother-in-law and my grandmother and the lady up the street who is an old friend." Nevertheless, I fear I was a trifle unkind as I stand-offishly assured Alberto that I know a reasonably well-recommended gerontologist. Then Alberto explained to me that in this modest country, a doctor accepts virtually anybody, and I won't specify anybody who can pay, because maybe the patient or parent will pay with chickens or eye-glass frames. Exclusive medical specialization with outrageous prices is not an option. To tell you the truth, my rebuffing his service was not due to mistrust of Alberto's skill; he is after all the best pediatric surgeon in the city. No, I have to confess, the problem is more like, how could I be his teacher, his superior in English, so intelligent and with beautiful eyes, plus a generation older to boot, and still retain my dignity when he examined my flagging corpus. It was vanity.

One Monday morning when I woke feeling seriously ill I tried to call Alberto's number to cancel class, but as often as not the telephones don't work, and it didn't. So he showed up on time at the gate. George went out and informed Alberto that la maestra was ill, and Alberto asked if he could see me. "Sure," I said, supposing he would greet me and leave.

I was in bed fully clothed, but since the covers were pulled up Alberto could see only my blouse which does look like a pajama top, I don't know why I bought it. I was holding my head and moaning while smiling cheerfully and the three of us set about joking while I suffered abdominal agonies. But wait a minute, Alberto was doing the doctor thing! He asked if I had vomited, if I had diarrhea, if I had eaten street food. He asked if I had a fever and George bounded into the bathroom to retrieve the fever thermometer which Alberto instructed me to place in my axillary, no, under the blouse. He asked if George had a blood pressure machine and George found his old one and inserted batteries and together they carefully ascertained my blood pressure was normal. Alberto wanted me to open wide and say "Aaah" and George quick as a wink had the batteries out of the blood pressure device and tucked into a nearby flashlight. My throat was clear.

Soon Alberto declared that I was experiencing a toxic reaction to something I had eaten. He gazed into my beautiful eyes and asked if I wanted him to bring medicine; his office was right around the corner and he would return immediately. Feebly, I nodded.

When he came back Alberto handed me a box of pills to quiet the stomach pain, and a small bottle of banana-flavored liquid sulfa compound. George fetched a spoon. Being somewhat larger than your average infant I swallowed a double dose. That stuff is vile.

On Wednesday, next class day, I was afoot, outfitted with mascara and a dictionary; the coffee was hot. Alberto didn't come. Finally, when his class time had passed he appeared at the gate to inquire after my health. It seems he had to go pay his auto excise tax; it was the very last day. Since I happen to know that Alberto, with Mexican disregard for the niceties, often doesn't bother with his driver's license, I could only be impressed. As for my illness, I was clearly improved, and in fact, I told him, I simply couldn't swallow any more banana syrup. Nor the pills either. "Fine," he replied, that was fine, and left me to my next student. Thus ended my worst illness of the year.

When Alberto arrived on Friday, I was watching to see if his attitude toward me had undergone a change—where formerly I was his beautiful intelligent teacher, was I now just another faltering elder? But if he ignored my health, would I become pettish for his lack of concern? Fortunately George had just gone off for a run up the local hill and when he returned the moments of magic intimacy vanished—Alberto loves to pretend we have an "understanding" which is hidden from George. George and I have an understanding which we try to keep hidden from Alberto, whom George refers to as my boyfriend, but whom I now refer to as my doctor. I remember the old wisecrack my mother loved, "I'm very sorry I can't come to work today, I'm in bed with the doctor." And she often was.

Do you see how this relates to house calls? Patients in the USA are wise not to regret them unless the patient is willing to crawl into a cradle and eat banana syrup. As for romance with a pediatric surgeon, there's more than one kind of Valentine.

baptism and beds for dogs

Our street is lined with some small shops, and outside one in particular hangs a sign that translates as "Beds for Dogs. Small Dogs, Medium Dogs and Large Dogs."

I am pondering the meaning of this. Well, first, people keep dogs; the animals dwell unhappily on the rooftops, where they pace back and forth and gaze anxiously down on the passers-by. Some bark, so I suppose they are guard dogs.

This brings point two, which is "affluence"; in quotation marks because affluence, all affluence, is relative. However, certain Oaxaqueños have sufficient household goods to require the guard services of roof dogs, and these dogs must be given some care, such as a Small, Medium or Large Bed.

And third, our neighbor is a small business entrepreneur, a capitalist of the style in Oaxaca, who keeps the shop open seven days a week, 10:00–2:00; 4:00–9:00. This business person is presumably earning some sort of living from the sale of dog products: food, beds, collars. I say "some sort" because the average per capita income in Oaxaca falls below the legal minimum wage, which is $3.00/hour American.

A glimpse of the dog bed business connects in my thoughts to the big socio-cultural questions we have of late been pondering: i.e., capitalism, and the meaning of communality. It's about sharing. Or nor sharing.

Our landlady kindly invited us to a family event at which her uncle served as baptismal godfather to two girls, ages five and nine, whose parents live in a small town called Zaachila, a Zapoteca town in the hands of the conservatives. The parents are both teachers, and the cards referred to them as Profesor and Profesora. Let me explain the cards. Each guest was given an ivory-colored occasion-card as a souvenir, with a coin of one or two pesos, based on the importance of the recipient I believe; the godmother received two pesos but I, an unknown guest of a guest, received one. These cards show on the back-side a precious painting of a cherub or saint or angel; on the front they are engraved with the names of the children, dates of births and baptism, the professor parents. And of course the taped-on coin.

The post-baptismal fiesta took place in a dirt patio, fenced with high cement walls. Standing outside the wall, with its painted advertisements and anonymous stone, I could not guess the size of the enclosure—big enough to hold tables and chairs for about two-hundred fifty guests, plus the two bands and the loudspeakers, themselves gigantic black oblongs whose pulse initiated throbbing ribs, and deafness in my ears. But never mind about the bands and the noise, here comes the food. I was seated between the landlady's college-student son, home from law-school in Mexico DF, for the Christmas holiday, who noticeably didn't eat, and the godmother/aunt.

Everyone was first served bread and hot chocolate, traditional. Break the bread, dunk it into the chocolate. Along with the breads each family was handed two plastic bags, one yellow, one white. These were for taking home the uneaten bread, tortillas or meat; one doesn't waste food. Certainly one doesn't rudely disdain it. The guests knew the customs, and George and I were informed. After the bread and chocolate came the macaroni soup in its plastic bowl, and after the soup the main dish, a hunk of brown meat served with side portions of avocado paste and refried beans. Sodas, beers, rum and coke for those who wanted it. The aunt seized my plate and ate the avocado and beans I could neither eat nor carry. We bagged our bread and meat. We left early due to the noise level, but I'm guessing that a sweet dessert brought the meal to an end. That's a lot of food for two hundred fifty people, a lot of paper napkins.

Flies swarmed everywhere. The cooking house that I observed was the usual thatch-roof open hut. The residence itself was of stone, and seemingly of good size; we didn't enter. In the patio, the smell of animal manure prevailed. But the little girls skipped about in white and pink satin gowns with bouffant skirts, hair wreaths, belt sashes. Politely, accompanying their mother who wore a long strapless black dress, they went to each guest and shook hands or embraced. The bands played in turn, one stationed at each end of the patio. And then the guests danced into the night.

Or so we supposed. Our landlady told us that the idea was both to have as many people as possible in attendance (George and I were bonus guests), and to spend as much money as possible, or at least appear to spend. This family may raise their own animals for butchering. Evidently their own extended family served the meal, cousins tripping about the dirt in city high heels, wielding heavy platters of tortillas and beef. Lined up at the long tables people sat quietly; the music's volume prevented any chatter. Nevertheless there was little of the intermingling one would expect among family or old friends, nor the convivial meeting and greeting of strangers. Nor were most specially dressed. It seemed to me a show of dutiful attendance for the guests. But it was a show of affluence for the hosts. So then I thought about the northwestern Indians of the US and Canada who showed their affluence by lighting a great bonfire and throwing all their goods into it; or maybe giving gifts of such value that reciprocity broke their neighbors. It was the idea of breaking your neighbors' heart—or balls—with munificence that struck me in Zaachila. But of course they were sharing their happiness and their bountiful food.

The Oaxaca theorist Gustavo Esteva, who apparently suffers from "noble savage" syndrome, speaks of an impoverished town where the neighbors share food in socially ritualized exchanges. I remember my Bostonian mother, circa 1950, lilac hair and brocade dress, going to dinner parties and bringing food, and indeed returning with some other dish. George and I still never go to a private home for a party or dinner without bringing something to eat or drink. Who doesn't? Guests whose hosts are so rich it would look like an insult to bring a pint of Ben & Jerry's for dessert. We were told not to bring food to Zaachila, and we didn't.

Instead George brought a copy of "Comunalidad and Autonomía", plus a tape of radical music, because both are the work of a Zapoteca man, Jaime Martínez Luna. George wants to share, which for him takes the form of spreading radical awareness; how was he to know the parents are supported by the PRI government?

Sharing is so instinctive, or so I maintain, that it's difficult to corrupt. Intimate couples give food off their plates to each other, or put the fork directly into the mouth of the loved one, like a child is fed by his mother or a bird by its mother. We practice in kindergarten how to share, and when it's birthday time, bring a cake for all the kids. Funerals, new neighbors, holidays—we bring food; and just as at the fiesta in Zaachila, we take home in bright yellow plastic bags the leftovers urged on us by our hosts.

Capitalism is what made it possible for my father to raise his children. Capitalism is what made it possible for me to sell my services, and hence achieve economic independence when I needed it.

Capitalism is what makes it possible for George to share. Capitalism is also what distorts, what permits the wealthy to exert power or cruelty or both. I think the dog-bed fellow is a capitalist because someone else stuffs and sews those pillows, someone hovers inside the open doorway to sell them, perhaps his wife, Large, Medium or Small. I doubt he's sufficiently successful as a capitalist to be unkind. In Oaxaca, having a dog to guard your home is not a new concept, but having a bed for the dog is.

buying grape juice

Arturo pushed the metal handcart up the gentle slope toward Santo Domingo Church, leaning over the handlebars, tolerating the ache in his shoulders. He didn't quite expect to see tourists; the temperature had gone past 35 and the sun sat on his cap like a father's punitive hand. Now he was a father himself, and his son traveled with him selling. Where at this moment was young Arturo? On a parallel street, also pushing a too heavy cart of wine bottles. Arturo the elder grieved for the boy's fate, although the boy had attended school through secondario and prepa. That was better than most here in Oaxaca, but so much less than Arturo the elder had hoped for, that his boy would have a career better than traveling pushcart salesman.

The Arturos worked with another man, and together the three made a circuit from their home in Veracruz to buy grape juice on franchise in Aguascalientes, and then more in Puebla. The fat purple grapes, grown organically, yielded a deep sweet juice, bottled and sealed, labeled, transformed by God and much hard work, then packed into their small truck. Every two months Arturo the older and Arturo the son left home with their partner, who did not have to peddle on the streets because he owned the truck. Their circuit passed through Oaxaca to Morelia and back to Puebla for a new load, until the harvest was exhausted. Arturo the elder was exhausted. His brown face felt gritty, his eyes boiled. He pushed the cap off his forehead and perched on the stone wall in front of the church, letting his feet dangle.

Then he noticed the gringa also sitting on the wall, with her cane tilted between her knees as she rested in the freckled shade. He knew this woman. "On sale". He pointed to the bottles, "normally 80 pesos each but today they're three for 100." He took an open bottle and poured a communion cup's worth for her to taste.

"I know it's delicious" the old lady said, but she took it anyway, throwing it into her mouth like a shot of mezcal. She smiled. "But you know I can't carry these bottles, you will have to bring them to our house." As she pressed her back he eyed her, turning sideways on the wall to better analyze her posture.

"How long have you suffered this problem with your back?" he asked. "Did you fall?"

"Everyone falls in Oaxaca, the first year I lived here I fell three times. But never broke anything. The stone sidewalks are dangerous. Now I don't fall anymore. The back signifies old age."

An insect from the tree above had landed on his neck and he brushed the spot, and then rubbed it. She tilted toward him. "No, there's no bite. Just an ant, I think." His neck resembled the bark of the guaje tree, but of a redder color.

"Never broke a bone? Not your wrist?"

"Once I broke my eyeglasses. Never a bone."

"That is truly lucky. Are you rubbing your back with ointment?"

"Which ointment?"

"There is one of arnica and one of sabila. Either will do well.

First you take the ointment in your hands and rub it to make it warm, like this." He rubbed his hands together and then touched her arm. "You feel the warmth of my hands even without the ointment, madre?"

She nodded. His hands perhaps were warm because the temperature was 96, and only a fool like herself was dutifully limping through obligatory daily exercise. The man didn't walk for exercise, she well knew. His face showed fatigue, and the old woman had to restrain herself from addressing him as son. "What's your name?" she asked.

Arturo began to explain how to apply the ointment. "Don't press, you will do more damage," he said. "Only apply with tender fingers, from up to down, stroking as you stroke a fish to see if the skin indicates it is too long out of water."

The woman had never stroked a fish, but did not say so. "I understand," she nodded. "I have arnica. Tonight I will try this remedy".

"And then you will sleep well, madre. Tell me, madre, how long do you require to walk home? And then I will come with the bottles."

"Fifteen minutes," she said, knowing it would take Arturo, bottles and cart, five. She rose gripping the cane, and since he was watching her as she went, stood straighter. Her sunhat shielded her eyes as she moved from shade into the falling glare, and then, for no reason at all, she took it off and jammed it into her tote. Bareheaded, she could feel a slight breeze, and felt stronger.

When she arrived home she put away her things, and sipped some water before the doorbell sounded. Arturo stood at the gate. She took her shopping bag and went out, with the hundred peso note in her hand, and handed him the money through the fence before she opened the gate and set the plastic bag down in front of him.

"Put the bottles in. No, lying down like this", she corrected him. When she straightened up she could lift the bag to walk the six paces to her door. Arturo was already speaking to the neighbor, who also had bought the grape juice two months before. She remembered how they both commended the excellent juice, exchanging murmurs of pleasure. But her neighbor was poor, and could buy only one bottle at a time. Nevertheless it was a good sale for Arturo.

As the old woman carried the juice into her kitchen she thought to herself, but the next time he comes to town he'll remember me. He'll come directly here, and I'll tell him about the gringos who live on the other street. They surely will buy when I recommend this excellent grape juice.

She nodded to herself. Arturo left. His wheelbarrow ground a faint departing noise on the stone street.

Essays

puro tequio

On October 10 we went up to Juanito's apartment where he was serving birthday beer and paella on his roof. To get out onto the roof you climb through a tiny rock door like Alice in Wonderland and I whacked my skull, so I had to drink quite a bit of beer to quiet the pain. Anyway, we met this woman who is from Ixtlán, up past Guelatao in the Sierra Norte, and we planned to go up there in Juanito's car and visit Maria del Carmen's brother and other family members who live there. Then Juan went off to Mexico DF on some business, and tonight we walked over to Carmen's to see if the trip is on, but Carmen wasn't home. Her father-in-law took us to her grandfather's to call Carmen's other brother, but the other brother said Carmen won't be back until tomorrow, although nobody seems to know where she went. The grandfather's house, behind the usual iron garage-style doors and cement walls, is very Mexican middle class, with photographs of Hollywood perfect family members and framed architectural scenes, a big chair in front of the TV, a glass lamp made of stacked colored bubbles in the shape of a Christmas tree, and a china cabinet filled with stemware and cups. The bookshelf displays a book on women's health, sex, and the Golden encyclopedia; the refrigerator is comfortably at hand behind the dining room table. Best of all, the floor is a lovely tile mosaic, of eternal multicolored flowers.

We hope Maria del Carmen gets back and Juanito does too; we really want to go up to Ixtlán because I have renewed interest in checking out the communal politico-social system used so widely in Oaxaca, of Usos y Costumbres, Uses and Customs, which I think initially we applauded more on romantic faith than on any hard facts. Well, as in Chiapas, also highly indigenous, the system works fine. The hard facts may be bad.

A small man shook out his banner, Exigimos... (We Demand...) painted boldly on a piece of white cloth. He placed it onto the stones of the sidewalk. He lay down on the cloth and fell asleep. This was the second day of the protest. I stationed myself on one side of Llano Park and George went to the other.

San Pablo Güila is a town of Usos y Costumbres in the Oaxaca mountains. The system of voluntary work for the community in San Pablo Güila requires four days of unpaid labor, called tequio, per week per man, and, as is common, the cargo (responsibility) for management of the town falls to chosen men who for one year at a time fulfill this cargo without salary.

Five thousand men and women marched briskly around four sides of the park across from the Chamber of Deputies. Various banners demanded government money for potable water, education, sewage treatment, roads, etcetera: in other words, the community's needs.

Tomasa, her hair westernized with henna and wearing stretch pants and sneakers, leaned against one of the trucks loaned to the demonstration. The trucks too are tequio. Tomasa stood on duty as First Aid dispenser although she's a midwife. First Aid consisted of aspirin and a swallow of water. The demonstrators, sleeping at night under the trees, brought only tortillas for food. There are no bathroom facilities nor drinking water. As usual, the park stinks.

Tomasa speaks Spanish well, along with Zapoteca. Most of the protesters speak Zapoteca - one of the six different versions —although they live in a region designated Mixte. While George was getting an idea of the geography of the district of Tlacolula, and within that, the municipality of Matatlán, and within that, the Agencia of San Pablo Güila with 4,800 people, and beyond that, its many rancherias which each support from 80 to 300 people without electricity, telephone or running water, I brought Tomasa a gift of six liters of bottled water and two more boxes of aspirin, and began to chat.

"So it's puro tequio," says Tomasa, nothing but work for the common good, no cash. How then could people obtain even the minimum necessary for bettering the infrastructure? But yes there is money. Oh, yes, it was sent down from the state government to the municipio of Mazatlan, where officials work for salaries. The pipeline stopped there. Tomasa did not say the funds were stolen, but those people are used to cash income, and the money came no nearer the Agencia of San Pablo Güila.

Another version is that the money actually went to Matatlán as bribes before the election, to officials who were supposed to get out the vote. They didn't. But how to disguise several millions of pesos required some ingenuity, such as claiming it was money designated by the government for civic improvements. Live with that, you rascals. The protesters are here to demand that the government force Matatlán officials to hand over the promised funds for water, schools and sewage.

Puro tequio also means that, according to Tomasa, 80% of the men migrated to the US, and sustain their duty to San Pablo Güila with remittances. The statistics we usually hear for Oaxaca men gone to the US for income is 60%, so this area perhaps is harder hit. The soil will not produce enough to support a growing population, and there is no other source of income.

A bigger tragedy for those who chose to migrate [within Mexico] is that in a great number of families, "the poverty increases because not all find well-paid or secure jobs", according to Ricardo Díaz Cruz, State Coordinator for the National Program for Agricultural Workers (Coordinador Estatal del Programa Nacional de Jornaleros Agrícolas).The phenomenon of migration, he explained, is not a choice, "people are fleeing, the migratory flow increases because there's no other way to survive. And on the other hand, the greater tragedy for the migrants is that their conditions of poverty don't improve. Often in this migration there are human losses, debts, and then the poverty is reinforced. In other cases families are destroyed and that generates more insecurity. The emigration generates and deepens poverty."

Díaz Cruz , responsible for PRONJAG, a branch of SEDESOL, observed that despite government efforts, "more Oaxaqueños seek other sources of income, jobs and education. Now, as a new phenomenon, day laborers are leaving the principal cities for the farming areas..."

Previously the migration was exclusively from rural zones. In the last few years it's from populated districts, from the poor neighborhoods, from the "cities of Oaxaca, Huajuapan, Loma Bonita, Tuxtepec, Tehuantepec, and Pochutla the population is leaving to become agricultural day labor."

Sadly, he said, there is no great change in the country to generate employment. Development was prioritized toward aiding large businesses and tourism, abandoning the micro and small businesses that could have generated more jobs.

He estimated about 100,000 families work at day labor in different parts of the republic each year, not only to agricultural areas in the north of the country but also to Chihuahua, Jalisco, Morelos, San Luis Potosí, Veracruz, and Michoacán.

The affected municipalities, he added, are not only the classic ones: Coatecas Altas, San Cristóbal Amatlán, San Miguel Mixtepec, Coycoyán de las Flores, and Juxtlahuaca; now there are other surprises like Santa María Chilchotla (Teotitlán de Flores Magón), Pochutla, Tehuantepec, and Loma Bonita "and that is a message that things are not getting better".

(translated by Nancy Davies from "Noticias de Oaxaca")

George and I have been translating subtitles for an indigenous video about women working in income-producing cooperatives, for example with coffee and pigs. Tomasa's immediate response to the idea of women taking more responsibility was negative; it's not part of traditional culture. It took her about ninety seconds to get over that. She herself came into Oaxaca to train as a midwife; she sees women stepping out of their homes. Truly, since there's little choice, the women must share more of the responsibilities, and as the video women say, they're better at managing income; they don't drink it or waste it. Tequio in San Pablo Güila already includes women producing endless stacks of tortillas.

The folks from San Pablo Güila are in something of a bind, because the zócalo in front of the Oaxaca Municipal Palace is occupied by two camps already, one for the women of Loxicha wanting their political-prisoner husbands freed, and the other for Antorchistas, an anarchist group shamelessly soliciting government funds, and the hell with contradictions. (Later we were told the Antorchistas are fakes, actually in the employ of the PRI to divide campesinos and stir rivalries.) So the San Pablo Güila crowd resorted to using Llano Park, but today, the third day of their encampment, we saw they had been pushed to the back side of the park to accommodate another demonstration, of teachers demanding higher salaries. The teachers and their supportive students ignored the growing stench of piss and whatever, and blocked the street for a while, presumably to make perfectly clear that they could do so if they chose.

Oaxaca is a place where the radio announcer's traffic reports are a list of blockades. This morning as he reported on Llano Park's environs he claimed that Oaxaca has more demonstrations than any city in Mexico, than any city in the WORLD, and added rather plaintively, "The government can solve this: just give them the money!"

Unlike some US cities where a blockade evokes frantic response from cops in gear with guns, in Oaxaca they send small neat police officers to re-route the buses, taxis and cars; and the encampments, blockades and pissing in public parks continue undisturbed by the forces for law and order. Once in a while a man in a suit ambles out of the Chamber of Deputies and speaks to the crowd, ambles back inside where the spokesmen for whatever protest stoically wait for a resolution or at least a promise.

Tequio lasting four days in San Pablo Güila, I supposed the demonstrators would rotate, but 4,800 is the whole town. So it's puro tequio nothing but tequio, all the way.

Our trip to Ixtlán came on November 11. It was after dark when Juanito, his friend Desirée and George and I piled into Juan's car to pick up Maria del Carmen and her eight year old daughter Mai Lan. Finally! But first we have to stop at the local store to buy water, ham, cheese and canned tuna to supplement the bread, fruit, cheese, almonds and raisins George and I already packed. And then we had to buy gas.

Well, off we go, up into the Sierra Madre del Norte, with Juan driving about thirty miles per hour over the rutted roads on the hairpin turns in the dark. As we entered Ixtlán Carmen wanted us to stop first at the new museum in the town square, to see what her brother has achieved. The museum formerly was the Municipal Palace, now replaced with a spanking new building. And a basketball court. And a clinic. Ixtlán also sports a magic clock tower in which the clock, a technical masterpiece, actually rings and runs, mechanically, soundlessly within its deep stone fortress. And Ixtlán's crowning glory is the adjacent old church of gothic dimensions and motif, interior high gilt, now under repair for the tourist industry. Ixtlán has two hotels already...

Carmen's family consists of a sister and two brothers who are both biologists. The one responsible for rescuing the old municipal building and having it renovated, turned it into a biological museum housing the town's collection of flora and specimens of the enormous bio-diversity of the region. But the museum was locked, since by now it was almost ten o'clock. Undaunted, Carmen, as soon as we drove through the metal door into her family's premises, showed us the adobe structure at the rear. Open Sesame, it's filled with computers and files; this brother works for SEMARNAP, the government organization responsible for monitoring the forests, agricultural areas, environment, etc. (SEMARNAP, the good guys in Oaxaca, are also responsible for reforestation efforts in Chiapas which disguise military encroachment: the soldiers who hi ho hi ho all day plant trees and build roads. Worse, the reforestation, instead of being native woods, serves the international paper companies with fast-growing eucalyptus, a tree which diminishes soil and water resources.)

Well wait a minute. Here we are inside the walls of Carmen's home. The structure is two stories of mixed brick, adobe and cement block, constructed around the patio occupied by two cars as well as Juan's. Each sub-family, of grandparents, sister and two brothers, has a suite. The grandparents moved to Oaxaca city, and so a bedroom upstairs is empty for George and me. That painted-cement room contains a double bed, a table, a single bed, a 1999 calendar, and an assortment of child's toys, empty plastic containers, cardboard boxes and mold. Next to the room is a non-functioning bathroom; then another suite, where the sister, husband, seven-month old baby and the baby's fourteen year old baby-sitter and maid of all work live. Decorating the outside patio on this level a lot of baby laundry waves, strung on clothesline.

Downstairs in this same side of the building is the room in which Juan and Desé will sleep, a Mexican-style bathroom (no toilet seat, no tank cover, occasional sink water, buckets for flushing or bailing as the situation may demand), a dim unused huge dining room, and a kitchen with no windows and no sink—the sink is outside in the patio.

We park our food offering in the kitchen. Everyone is starved. Sandwiches in a hurry. The cats prowl for mice and dogs come and go. One dog, a handsome black Lab, is totally blind from birth. He gets around, but not quickly.

So now it's time to go out with the local gang. Carmen is clearly attached to her hometown friends, several of whom seem to be university students, also home for a weekend. The moon is full, with the Mexican rabbit leaping upward and the American Man smiling down. We drift down the quiet street and climb up into a field in front of an abandoned house. Quick work makes a fire of old wood, surrounded by stones to prevent the fire spreading. The night's cool, we all wear jackets. The blind dog bumps into me, and stands poised sniffing the wind. Some youngsters perch on the abandoned cement horse trough. Others drag a log close to the fire. A guitar appears, and marshmallows to roast. Singing round the campfire. It's Juan who wants to feed the fire, to keep going the talk and laughter. Juan was thirty-six on that night of paella and my whacked head. He's no kid. But lost. Seeking roots and routes that never were his; his ancestry is Spanish, not indigenous. His skin doesn't darken despite hours in the sun; his brown hair neither darkens nor uncurls. He asks each of the young people about speaking Zapoteca (no) knowing the old stories(no) planning to live in Ixtlán - no. Carmen, who clearly loves her home, talks of emigrating with her husband and Mai Lan to Canada.

In the morning I woke at the sound of work in the street, Sunday morning radio music, somebody whacking something metal. Six A.M. Ugh. Four hours sleep. At eight I went out and watched the girl maid sweep dirt and an empty plastic bottle down the stairs. She leaned over the porch rim and called to her friend below, and then finished her chore and disappeared. The blind dog and I went out of the compound into the cobblestone street. I returned alone without the dog. At ten Juan got up and he and Carmen set off in search of a guide to the forests.

The guide's name is César, and we're his first clients in four months. Private business. He drives a pick-up truck, (we pay for gas) and George and I as old folks ride with him in the cab while the rest of the group (we've acquired another friend) bounce on the hard open metal bed of the truck.

Ixtlán owns the forests as communal property, and logs it very carefully under the watchful vigilance of SEMARNAP. The computer room is recording tree ages, sizes, numbers and self-generating new growth; species and their Latin names and local purposes. A previously unknown species of oak is named rodriguez, Carmen's brother.

We go up up up. Nine thousand plus feet. Finally on foot, César explains the four forest ecologies: the cloud forest, high forest, dry and temperate. We stand on Mexico's continental divide. The pine-trees are stunted by the winds. Clouds throw their shadows on the surrounding mountains, the cool air frets our clothes. One can't help feeling the winds as gods; they are ever-present and pulling toward the four corners of heaven.

Down we go for a picnic surrounded by insects, under a roof-shelter. The cloud forest level is shrouded in a type of plant reminiscent of Longfellow's description of Nova Scotia: "bearded with moss and in garment green." The humidity in the air condenses and runs down the trees to supply moisture in the dry months; the road is muddy. Lupine, yellow daisies. Something which seems to resemble mountain laurel and azalea, raspberries. Six varieties of oak. César says that from this spot one could walk five days before exiting forest.

Ixtlán is rich.

We drive down toward the town where a trout farm, also communal, raises fingerlings into very respectable dinners, each fish roasted in aluminum foil, served by the men who pull the fish from their tanks. A chill river tumbling down from the mountains makes this enterprise possible. We were eight at the wooden trestle table; the bill for fish soup, trout and a bottle of soda each, came to 308 pesos total: $30. César says that on a weekend they clear about three thousand each day. Not much yet. But growing.

As we exit the fish farm and drive back toward Carmen's home, a billboard alongside the road reads, "THIS TOWN IS COMMUNAL PROPERTY. NO LAND IS BOUGHT OR SOLD."

Two examples of Usos y Costumbres. Two towns, one in terrible condition, the other thriving. As in Chiapas, it all has to do with ownership of natural resources. The soil in San Güella is exhausted, the trees disappeared, and the men followed after.

What is very clear to me is that Ixtlán people are not into "Home Beautiful" arrangements yet. But there's a new furniture store opened across from the church. Cars for the middle-class, and some kids go down to the university. Fourteen year old maids, dropped out of school. Maria del Carmen, city resident with a husband who works in a bank, hoping for a chance to leave what she most loves.

We're back in Oaxaca exhausted. To Carmen I say, a thousand thanks for your wonderful hospitality! Which of course she accepts with a huge smile. Mai Lan waves goodbye and they disappear behind one of the huge metal doors in Oaxaca. Juan heads the car toward our street.

looking behind walls

October 8, 2000

It's easy to think of Mexico, at least southern Mexico where we are, as somehow goofy. Clownish. Every night some small band marches down the street tootling away, followed by bigger-than-life papier maché puppets. Inside the puppet skirts, or pantaloons for guy puppets, sneakers and jeans twirl and bob. The male puppets wear fine black moustaches painted on their pink paper faces. Pink circles adorn the cheeks of the lady puppets. Behind the puppets comes the parade, for a church or a sisterhood or a union, all the same. The women carry flowers on their heads. The men carry flowers in their arms, or banners, or saints. Interchangeable. Behind the marchers a group of miscellaneous participants tote cellophane torches. A man expert in tossing fireworks and rockets tosses them. Bang. Bang. How can one take it seriously?

Fresh foods and world-class concerts cost about one-tenth of what we pay in the USA, a reasonable restaurant dish can be had for $3.50. Today Oskar told me he read that Oaxaca is one of Mexico's most expensive cities. The local newspaper's headline claims Oaxaqueños may consume 70% of their daily requirements for nutrition.

The bride exits the church dressed in a traditional USA white satin gown, with bridesmaids in high heels and a troop of serious flower girls in long dresses. A band plays at the church door.

The bell rings for trash collection. Oh, this week no collection. The truck is broken. A horn blats for gas. Run out and buy a tank of gas. Men roll down the streets hollering Aaaaaagua. Run out and get some water. How can this be serious?

It's the vampire effect. In a horror movie, you know that no matter how silly vampires may be in reality, in one's own reality they're just outside the window. In Mexico, sunny-day vampires, if such exist. By which I mean, some not so wonderful and timeless fate lurking. Stone saints who live on cathedral heights wave off the vampires, the pigeons, the bats. Lots of churches, lots of stone, lots of saints. Benedictions fall like the saints themselves fall in earthquakes. They leave the vampires untended.

In our walled-in patio the odor of rain hitting dust greets me. About five o'clock the cleared sky suddenly clouded over, thunder rumbled. A lizard falls with a sharp plop from a wall to the cement patio. Or maybe it was the brilliant orange flower that plopped off a tree? The startled lizard gathers its wits and heads back to the wall. As it starts to climb, raindrops begin, and here's that odor, that odor of wet dust. It lasts just a few minutes, and then we're awash...

I become more aware of walls, through which small busy men pass buckets of sand. Looking into the area beyond, I see there must have been a structure, now gone. The lot is cleared, but the wall stands; there's no reason tear down a perfectly good wall. No machines, no Cats and back-hoes; construction is done by hand. Also, there are no basements. So why should the wall come down? The construction work resembles bailing the ocean. Somehow ominous,

not threatening, but ominous in its reminder of eternity, in wait like
a vampire. There's no time pressure when all work is wrested manu-
ally: next week, next month, next year. The Oaxaca gentleman who
presides at state band concerts and announces every couple of weeks
the same history of Oaxaca, its music and culture, to the audience,
this fine man breathlessly announced the decision—a big political
decision—to fix the clock in the Catedrál tower, broken for decades.
That was the fourth such announcement, and only one month ago;
the black iron hands haven't moved.

And yet this odd timelessness is belied by change. The sense of
change is everywhere. The encampments demanding restitution, ac-
tion, liberation, dismissal, are lengthy and determined. Campesinos
spread cardboard pallets on the sidewalks and sleep. They build fires
on stone circles in front of the municipal palace and cook. They separate their camp from the camp of the women demanding release of
the Loxicha prisoners of 1996. They block streets and use loudspeakers to make their demands heard.

Intellectuals distinguish Mexico Profundo from Mexico Imagi-
nario. Imaginary Mexico is a first world country, or, like the book title
reads, *First World Ha Ha Ha*. Daily life involves small details - endless
trucks with oranges, endless women hauling tortillas door to door,
bumblebees as big as your hat and the neighbor's bilingual parrot hollering "asshole!"—the context in which Mexico changes hides behind
walls.

I spoke with my young friend Oskar who has begun his first year
at University Benito Juarez. He tells me frankly that if he wanted to
discuss what is happening in his country nobody at school, no professor, no student, could do so. They give him the information he needs,
the courses he must cover for his major in Communications; communications, it seems, empty of content. He explained that young
people know about birth control but think pregnancy won't happen;
they form rival gangs who snub each other for wearing name brand

clothes or not, for being poor or less poor; they're atheists and disregard the Catholic Church; they begin work young; they fight on their own turf. Rarely do they participate in the protests of their elders. That's not where their heads are at. Not yet.

So I thank Oskar for his insights. A population explosion which the government has little success damping surpasses Mexico's resources. Public political battles flare over abortion rights; public ads on TV and movie theater walls promote the use of condoms. Newspapers denounce the decline in education (have we heard all this before?) and we read scrawled on intact walls slogans denouncing the government's role in the 1968 massacre of student protesters. Yesterday I decoded a graffiti message: "Blessed is Chaos, it shows that something is happening."

The indestructible walls, of banks and tumbled tourist shops, of hotels and crumbled restaurants, get defaced repeatedly, or should we say adorned. It crosses no one's mind that these walls through which men pass buckets of sand by day, by night serve as communication systems easily outstripping everything Oskar learned today in school.

Riding the bus to a town outside the city I spoke to a pleasant-looking woman wearing the common apron and clutching a bag of bread. Is the farmland we pass private or communal? "Communal," she replied. The produce is sold in Oaxaca City. I said, Well, the town must be run by Usos y Costumbres (Uses and Customs). She confirmed that observation, but the surprise her face clearly expressed indicated to me that this fact is unknown to foreigners and tourists, although it's public, government-published knowledge that most of Oaxaca's 547 municipalities use the traditional system of governing, something akin to town meeting. Corn and beans were growing beneath the backdrop of cloud-strewn mountain.

Communal lands don't mean there aren't caciques, another secret. But those protests, those demands—whereas in days of old someone might have murdered such a fellow, now the men come to the Chamber of Deputies to demand the miscreant be removed from office. Does that work? Depends on the level of political corruption.

Guerrillas in the mountains are a secret, too. Oskar knows about the existence of the EPR. He reads their messages on the walls. He knows the income of many campesinos may be less than thirty pesos per week. Oscar, I asked, why are they fighting? What do they want?

But that he didn't know.

matrimony

We got a call from our friend Jonathan. He's planning to marry Ana María in January, and of course we're invited to the wedding in Colonia Reforma at the Church of Our Lady of the Poor.

Well, not so fast, Buckaroo. First, Jonathan wanted to know, would George and I be so kind as to be his character witnesses? Before the officiating priest will perform the religious wedding, two witnesses each for bride and groom must swear and sign that the prometidos are not already married, nor have undeclared children, nor sell drugs.

Our first task was to find the restaurant where Jonathan and Ana María would breakfast with us, before we headed for the parish office.

No point in a Bostonian complaining about a lack of street signs. We asked eight or nine people, and after circling the area for fifteen minutes, located the restaurant. Jon sat alone off to one side under an umbrella. He looks nice for a guy in his forties—thinning but not bald, dashingly dressed in a Mexican white embroidered cotton shirt. I was glad I goosed George to shed his tee-shirt (torn at the shoulder) and don a respectable front-button shirt. But where was Ana María? Late. She has la gripa, which could mean anything from a cold to flu. She'll come.

The main floor of the restaurant was arranged for a big private affair, with decorated tables set for sixty-five. This is where Jon and Ana will host their wedding dinner, so we enjoyed a preview. A kids' play area sat on one side of the patio. The place looked small for one hundred fifty, but Jon doesn't seem concerned.

We settled down to listen to Jonathan's account of the hours of inevitable coming and going he invested to obtain the trámites necessary for the civil wedding, a supplement to the religious one. After forty-five minutes Ana showed up, looking feverish but attractive, in matching lime green sweater set and filmy skirt, bare unshaved legs and high heels.

While we drank our coffee, the restaurant brothers dismantled the place settings for sixty-five and re-arranged the tables, due to a small error—the private party was the next day, not today. We enjoyed a nice breakfast with the restaurant to ourselves; the waiter bent the sun umbrella to place George in the shade. That's not a trivial chore.

Finally we strolled around to the church, where we met Ana's parents, both teachers. They call Jonathan "Yony." I asked Jon what his mother-in-law–to-be's name is, but he said he actually didn't know, since he never addresses her as anything but Maestra. I learned her name is Queen Mary, and the Maestro is Wille. Queen Mary and I chatted as older women will, discussing clothing and customs, and finally Queen Mary asked if George and I, as a couple, would participate in a traditional dinámica, at her house two days before the wedding. Unlike a shower, the dinámica explicitly requires twelve couples bearing symbolic gifts. Ours was to be a clock or watch of some kind, to remind the bride to be timely in performing her household chores.

Finally it was our turn for the interview with the priest, a pleasant fellow in a blue plaid flannel shirt, seated behind his glass-topped desk.

First, we swore with right hands raised that we would tell the truth. How long had we known Jon? How long have George and I been married? Immediately George blurted we've been living for ten years in Unión Libre, information the priest politely ignored.

You should understand that George and I dwell at opposite ends of the liars' spectrum. George will never, I will always. And we already promised Queen Mary to stand in as one of the twelve married couples. The priest asked, Que religión tiene? George thought the priest was asking for George's religion, and I could sense wheels grinding while he figured out how to declare he's an atheist. The priest looked alarmed too; he sensed it coming and really didn't want to know. He shouted the question several times, el jóven, el jóven, el jóven, finally pointing to a picture of Jonathan; finally we understood. Unfortunately, we didn't know the answer, since among American friends, unless they're Born Again or Jewish, the question hardly ever arises.

I thought he was Catholic, I asserted, and the priest pointed to Jon's testimony, He says he's Episcopalian!

If he says so, it must be true, he's a very honorable man! I shot back, hoping that would save the day. I think the priest simply gave up, and we signed our names and were released.

Ana needed to go home to bed, and Queen Mary invited us to walk along to her house on Palmeras, a block away, to see where it's located, so we'd absolutely know, for the dinámica. Wille had instructed us to arrive en punto, a time virtually unknown in Mexico.

Ana María disappeared promptly once we went inside, and since we declined a coke Queen Mary escorted us to the other side of a patio fence where her son and grandchildren live. She invited us to the Christmas fiesta her son would host for the children to break a piñata. Jonathan will notify us of the day and hour. I could hear

George's brain working again, this time on how he could get some piñata candy.

This is your house, Queen Mary told us, in the traditional way. She wrote on a piece of paper for me, Reyna María Arreola Rodriguez, the address, the telephone number, the hour and day of the dinámica—no way to get lost. Wille, along with Ana, vanished, and I was feeling the fatigue that results from chatting and laughing in a foreign language. We thanked her as best we could, said goodbye to Jon, and took off.

The walk back to our apartment was much shorter because we knew the way. I felt enormously better when I awoke from my nap.

Only three more events to get through, to see Jonathan safely married.

On Saturday, not knowing the wedding fairy had us in thrall, we went off to Huayapán. We went innocently, just to travel like the idle rich—to any place by bus, for three pesos. The tiny town of Huayapán was recommended by a friend who loves the traditional ways of Oaxaca. We disembarked behind the church, and came round to the empty zócalo.

The tiny square enclosed on one side the local jail, a cage, inside which a man was howling, "Señ-o-o-o-r! Aye, Señ-o-o-o-o-r!" Neither the Lord nor anyone else responded to his wail. The other side of the zócalo is a roofed and concrete mercado, entirely empty; the third side, the municipal buildings, were all shut. With no other option, we strolled down two or three dirt streets lined with houses of adobe and sleeping dogs. A woman passing stopped us and invited us to go to a wedding, taking place in just a few minutes, in the church. She asked where we were from, accepted us as foreigners, and said the wedding was the place to be—indeed, the only show in town.

George and I circled the dogs and unpaved streets, admiring a few arches, very nicely constructed of the same adobe brick. By now steeple bells were clanging, so we ascended the sloping street and made our way into the church.

These churches! Virtually every one bears a sign proclaiming a Cultural Patrimony restoration. They are so old. This one of Huayapán lost not only its paint on the interior domed ceilings and side murals, but also suffered structural damage in the last earthquake. The many saints appeared in good shape, though, well-clothed and surrounded by flowers and candles. We entered a pew, and sat trying to avoid kicking the kneeling rail.

At the front stood the bride and groom. The congregation numbered perhaps forty, in day clothes, so jeans were not out of place. Four guys who also sang played wedding music on guitars. Little children scampered through the aisle while the priest told us the bride was a Huayapán girl but the fellow a stranger from San Pablo Etla, at least fifteen miles away. Nevertheless they found love.

To show what love can accomplish, the priest baptized two toddlers during the wedding ceremony—he doesn't come often to this tiny parish. Then vows were exchanged. Next to us an old woman wearing the usual cotton checkered delantal tied over her dress, kneeled and stood and kneeled and stood, nimble in a way which astonished me. If she had arthritis it didn't show, but goiter did, climbing her throat in front of her thin gray braided hair. If she was poor—and I believe they're all poor—that didn't show either, because when the collection plate came around she called out to the man holding it, who might have passed her by; she took her peso from her delantal pocket and tossed it in.

I wondered what age she was. Often it's better not to know.

As the ceremony seemed interminable, we stepped out to the courtyard where fireworks were exploding. The usual gaggle of small boys gazed upward enchanted as rockets banged and gray flakes rained down. The band sat ready on the stone walls, holding their cornets and tubas. Finally the priest appeared and sped away in a green

Dodge. The four-man guitar band tumbled out of the back door into a waiting truck. A boy neatly dressed in a green sweater came round and offered rice from a basket, for us to throw at the hapless couple who now moved into the waiting sunshine. They flinched; the bride turned her back to protect her face, the groom shielded his eyes with his hand. Rice pelted them like hail. The band played.

An ordinary-appearing couple.

They set off on foot, the bride lifting her traditional ivory satin dress above the dust. The groom wore a gray suit jacket over unmatched gabardine pants. Behind them trailed family and friends. The band was cheerful, and so were we, following along uninvited. Nobody minded us, and after three blocks the wedding party turned a corner toward their waiting festivities, and we continued along the main road. We met the bus returning to Oaxaca, and waved it to a stop. That's also traditional, since bus stops in the country are wherever the traveler stands. Through the bus window I could make out in the rolling distance the blue eye of one Huayapán dam.

We've been to a 2001 wedding, and the 2002 wedding is approaching. I suppose Jon's and Ana's will be a classier affair. But the basics are the same. They seem to want to be married.

Part Two: Well, first, the word dinámica was completely unknown to other Mexican friends. After I described it as best I could, they nodded thoughtfully andreplied, yes, a family blessing on the couple. A bendición.

On the evening of the event we arrived at five punctually, but others of course were late, including the brother of the groom, who is not even Mexican. Eventually, the master of ceremonies began, with a speech on the importance of love and marriage, and then a recorded song in praise of eternal love, and then another speech and finally he signaled for bringing of gifts. Each gift was also accompanied by a "lesson" printed in Spanish, with a place at the bottom to sign our names.

The gifts one by one were carried forward to the waiting couple seated at the front of the room. I felt a sudden urge there to say "doomed couple", but they really seemed okay. Ana wore a white be-ribboned shift with a lace underskirt, very Mexican. As the evening wore on, she looked more than a tiny bit tired.

We all sat in chairs along the walls, facing the couple. George and I stood while he read out our gift's lesson. After the gifts came the blessing. More words from the master of ceremonies, and now they were translated into English by the padrino, Jon's good friend and sponsor, down from the US for the wedding. Audience members made speeches on the importance of marriage, and those were trans-lated. I believe I counted ten or so before I quit. Wisely, the padrino said that in the interest of finishing at a reasonable hour, he would skip some, to translate later on for those who needed to know.

Then Queen Mary made a speech, and gave her blessings. All the women shed tears, and Jon was handed a kleenex, and so was Jon's brother, who apparently thought bachelor Jon would never marry. The brother assured us his wife (sitting beside his empty chair as he stood to speak) was beautiful and they were extremely happy.

It was clear this business of bendición is actually a family and community ceremony to impress on Jonathan that the marriage is for real—no skipping off to the USA and leaving behind a ravished bride.

The method of blessing is as follows: one makes the sign of the cross individually upon bride and groom, then using two hands, brings together their heads, until they touch.

Two hours later I was desperate to stand up, my back killing me on the little wooden chair. George and I got to our feet, and blessed the couple without making the sign of the cross. I hope it took any-way.

The bendición was followed by a buffet supper, with a disk

jockey to make sure the bride, groom parents, brothers and in-laws, god-parents, etcetera, etcetera, danced a waltz with bride, groom, and one another. Beer, champagne for toasting, good food—and then the genuine Mexican dancing erupted.

Around ten o'clock George and I left the party. There was no doubt it would go on without us.

Although I thought the bendición was a real fun ordeal, it hardly compared to the actual wedding. The service at Our Lady of the Poor mercifully began only fifteen minutes late, and was brief, only an hour and a half, and I felt cheered by the time we arrived at the restaurant for the party. Silly me.

Add one hundred fifty people, loud speakers, and repeat all the above.

We chatted with whomever we could over the noise. I admired the clothing of several people, men, women and children, who wore outfits made of manta, as the bride's dress was, only hers was scalloped and embroidered and carried a long train. Manta is cotton, but of a kind not seen in the US—heavy as cream.

Now a live band appeared, and mezcal, champagne, beer, and food which clearly was not the important part of the event. The blessing of the couple was repeated in another form: the bride placed wreaths on the heads of those who brought her into the world or helped her grow and learn—in fact, quite a lot of people. Again, the community clearly joined those two, never to be put asunder.

Ana's godfather twirled me around, George joined the line of men dancing around the groom who was tossed into the air by his friends; everybody danced together and separately. The bride's train was held up as she stood on a chair, to form an arch under which the dancing could snake. Some of the traditional antics struck me as verging on cruelty, but the bride held up well. The groom made a great show of taking off her garter, the bride threw the bouquet, all went according to plan. Once those miserable waltzes terminate, Mexican dancing is all-out.

At our table sat one other English-speaking person, and the "sister-cousin" of Queen Mary, and her family, one of whom is named Xicotencatl. Not that the family is Nawal, they're not, their mestizo mix is Zapoteco. Mercedes, the mother, just liked the name. I got on with Mercedes who shares a birth year with me, and we spoke of getting together for dancing lessons so I could better hold up my end of future Mexican festivities. I asked Mercedes if she knew if Jon and Ana Maria would have a honeymoon, but she was extremely happy and just shrugged. On my other side, the Canadian woman, who lives in Guatemala, confided in George's ear some of her tragic life. Meanwhile, George got on wonderfully with Xico until Xico was too drunk to speak. By then many others were no better off. The exhausted couple cut the cake.

Since nobody remained sober enough to talk to, and the loudspeaker blared near our table, once again we departed before the festivities ended.

If you're keeping tally, we spent (including meals) four hours getting Jonathan licensed, five hours getting him blessed, and eight hours getting him married.

Demonios, as we say in Oaxaca. The marriage must last to amortize our investment over the next fifty years.

On Sunday, the following morning, George and I went out with our camera, to goof around. In front of a small hotel hidden away on the side of the Oaxaca hillside George saw a set of stones protruding from the side of a wall. On top of the wall was the sidewalk, these were stairs. I took his picture as he climbed. We also noticed a car parked on the street in front of the wall. Written on it: Ana y Jonathan, reciente casado. George took out a piece of paper and wrote a note to put under the windshield wiper. "We were going to drop in to see you but thought you might be busy. Love, George and Nancy."

thanksgiving

It's quite easy to buy a cheese grater in Oaxaca, a flat made-in-China tin alloy rectangle with a handle, for no more than a couple of bucks. But I already have a cheese grater. It's somewhere, on route from Boston-New Jersey-California-Laredo-Nogales. And it might get here soon. So why buy another? The modern ones aren't that good anyway, and mine has diligently grated on, for at least fifty years.

It's also possible to buy Kraft grated Parmesan cheese, in a plastic container with a green cover with holes to shake out the cheese. Which I bought, for our spaghetti, for several years until this week when I experienced my grated cheese epiphany and decided Kraft grated cheese is not really cheese, it's chemicals in powder form. From here on, only pure Parmesan, imported from Italy and enveloped in fine black wax. Hence the need for a grater.

It's the night before Thanksgiving, and I'm thinking about how in my family days I would grate and chop, pare and cut, roll the crusts and stuff the birds, etcetera. Not being very good at expressing my affection verbally or physically, I relied on cooking one giant meal for the year's worth of nurturing. It remains my most sentimental and cherished holiday: myself as mother.

Here in Oaxaca many ex-patriots prepare a traditional Thanks-giving dinner, including cranberry sauce flown down in the luggage of snow-birds. Not us, though. I don't want to try to evoke that big early-winter family plus football game gathering, when I live with George in the warm sun. Oaxacans are succumbing to Halloween and Christmas, two absolutely poisonous commercial encroachments, but so far, no Thanksgiving. Even the American library will stay open, for those of us with no Thanksgiving spirit.

But I do have the spirit. I sallied out to our local Gigante, the to-be-avoided Oaxaca commercial supermarket, to bring home a nice piece of imported Parmesan, for tonight's spaghetti. I set about grat-ing it with a serrated knife. It took me about two hours; my forearm stiffened and my hand cramped. George mercifully ate the last inch. I'm dusted all over the front of my embroidered Mexican blouse with a fine pollen of Parmesan. The table is sprinkled, too; I sweep up cheese and deposit it into the empty Kraft container which George so sweetly cleaned off for me in anticipation of this event. I saved the container for three months, and finally, here it stands, to serve its destiny. In goes the Parmesan, like dust in the vacuum cleaner bag which I anticipate arriving soon. The spaghetti is boiling, the vegeta-ble sauce for it simmers with garlic and basil. George looks at me and remarks, I've never seen you so patiently preparing food. He didn't know me in my Thanksgiving days, and obviously forgot the year I cooked at his house, which certainly I have no intention of reminding him of. Instead I reply, I used to do it all the time, for Thanksgiving, fifteen hours of labor for thirty minutes of eating. Ah, says George, you miss Thanksgiving.

No, not a bit of it. What I miss is the act of cooking as a display of nurturing. Don't you notice, I say peevishly to George, that I chop and peel and cut and stir vegetables for you every damn night? This is more or less a lie; I do it a few nights per week, one night we eat out and on three we eat re-heated leftovers. It's not really nurturing, it's my half of our living agreement: I cook he washes.

Nevertheless, in reply to my surly assertion, he came around the table to kiss the back of my neck, the front being oily with cheese dust.

I don't know if it's better to give or to receive, when it comes to nurturing. Maybe it depends on who's cooking, and if you like spaghetti. I loved seeing grated cheese melted on hot sauce, unlike Kraft which sits in a sort of perky poison waiting the demise of the meal. But I have no intention of enduring two hand-paralyzing hours of grating again. I found my Thanksgiving moment, hecho a mano, like we say hereabouts, and now I'll wait for my grater to arrive, or if it never comes, I'll buy a new one, made in China.

About the Author

Nancy Davies has resided in Oaxaca since 1999. She's the author of personal commentaries dealing with the Oaxaca uprising of 2006. They were published on www.narconews.com and partially collected in book form as The People Decide. Other commentaries by Nancy Davies appeared on http://upsidedownworld.org, from 2008 until 2010.

In her past life Davies' poetry appeared in small and literary magazines. Her previously unpublished works, including poems, novels, essays, and vignettes will be progressively available on http://www.nmsdavies.com/, her "writer's selfie".